Love's

Lady Mimosa stood... wide and frightene... her breasts.

"So it was you who... touched me!" she gasped.

Now as she remembered how she had felt a man's hand move first down one side of her body, then the other, the colour came into her cheeks because she had been wearing so little at the time.

"Yes, it was I," Norton Field said, "and it was then it struck me that I might have arranged things differently, which is what I am going to do now."

"And... what is... that?"

Even as she asked the question, Mimosa shrank in fear from the answer. It would be something she did not wish to hear and she knew perceptively it would be horrible, degrading, and terrifying.

"What I intend to do," Norton Field said, "is to marry you..."

A Camfield Novel of Love by Barbara Cartland

———————————

"Barbara Cartland's novels are all distinguished by their intelligence, good sense, and good nature..."

—ROMANTIC TIMES

"...who could give better advice... than the world's most famous romance novelist, Barbara Cartland?"

—THE STAR

Dearest Reader,

Camfield Novels of Love mark a very exciting era of my books with Jove. They have already published nearly two hundred of my titles since they became my first publisher in America, and now all my original paperback romances in the future will be published exclusively by them.

As you already know, Camfield Place in Hertfordshire is my home, which originally existed in 1275, but was rebuilt in 1867 by the grandfather of Beatrix Potter.

It was here in this lovely house, with the best view in the county, that she wrote *The Tale of Peter Rabbit*. Mr. McGregor's garden is exactly as she described it. The door in the wall that the fat little rabbit could not squeeze underneath and the goldfish pool where the white cat sat twitching its tail are still there.

I had Camfield Place blessed when I came here in 1950 and was so happy with my husband until he died, and now with my children and grandchildren, that I know the atmosphere is filled with love and we have all been very lucky.

It is easy here to write of love and I know you will enjoy the Camfield Novels of Love. Their plots are definitely exciting and the covers very romantic. They come to you, like all my books, with love.

Bless you,

CAMFIELD NOVELS OF LOVE
by Barbara Cartland

Other books by Barbara Cartland

A NEW CAMFIELD NOVEL OF LOVE BY

BARBARA CARTLAND

Haunted

A JOVE BOOK

HAUNTED

A Jove Book/published by arrangement with
the author

PRINTING HISTORY
Jove edition/April 1986

ISBN: 0-515-08512-X

Jove Books are published by The Berkley Publishing Group,
200 Madison Avenue, New York, N.Y. 10016.
The words "A JOVE BOOK" and the "J" with sunburst
are trademarks belonging to Jove Publications, Inc.

PRINTED IN THE UNITED STATES OF AMERICA

Author's Note

AFTER fifteen years of war against Napoleon Bonaparte, many of the men returning to England, whatever their position in life, found peace more difficult to cope with than war.

Those with country estates found there was vast unemployment. The farmers were doing extremely badly after a bad harvest, and many country banks went bankrupt.

There was a general air of dissatisfaction and depression over the whole country. In London the Bucks and Beaux returned from the forces to the gaiety and pleasure that centred around the Prince Regent, but even he was getting older and there was not the *joie de vivre* there had been at the beginning of the century.

chapter one

1817

THE Marquis of Heroncourt watched the last of his guests walk down the long flight of stone steps from the front door to where carriages were waiting to carry them back to London.

They had all thanked him profusely for a most delightful visit, but Lady Isme Churton had come back to say in a soft voice which only he could hear:

"I shall be looking forward, dearest Drogo, to seeing you tomorrow night."

The Marquis smiled vaguely, and as if there were no need for him to reply Lady Churton ran down the steps with a grace for which she was famous and stepped into the last remaining carriage.

Then she bent forward to wave her gloved hand through the window. Her face, with its slanting eyes and provocative mouth, was framed by her fashionable and high-crowned and lace-trimmed bonnet.

The Marquis of Heroncourt waved in return, and then as the carriage moved off he turned to his last remaining guest, Charles Toddington, standing beside him, and said:

"Well, thank God that is over!"

Major Toddington's eyes twinkled.

"I had no idea, Drogo, you were feeling that the party had gone on too long."

"Far too long!" the Marquis said positively. "Never again, and I am serious, Charles, will I ask anyone, however attractive, to stay for a week!"

Charles Toddington laughed. Then he said:

"I thought you were being a little over-optimistic in supposing that even the most alluring of our Beauties would last that long!"

The Marquis walked through the marble hall, with its statues of gods and goddesses and a magnificent marble fireplace that had been specially sculpted for it.

Then he went through an open door which led into the small Library where he habitually sat when he was alone or with one of his more intimate friends.

He walked determinedly across the room to the window and stood looking out as if he had never before seen the formal garden with its yew hedges, its fountain, and unique topiary work.

Then he said, and his voice was harsh:

"It is ridiculous, absolutely ridiculous, that we should admit to being bored when we have just spent a week with not only the most acclaimed Beauties in the *Beau Monde* but also a number of men who are noted for their wit and talent to amuse."

Charles Toddington sat down in an armchair and crossed his legs.

"I agree with you, Drogo," he said, "and the fault obviously lies with us rather than with them. So the question we should be asking ourselves is, What is wrong?"

"I can tell you what is wrong," the Marquis said. "It is the monotony and the unutterable boredom of finding every day is the same as the last, with nothing unusual happening except that somebody has lost or won a fortune at cards, or a new face has cropped up like a mushroom in Piccadilly, which in a few days will be supplanted by another!"

Charles Toddington threw back his head and laughed.

"Quite poetical! At the same time, I know exactly what you are saying because I feel the same."

"You do?" the Marquis enquired. "Then tell me the reason why, and it seems incredible, I do not care if I never again set eyes on the people who have just left my house."

Charles's eyes twinkled.

"You will make an exception where Isme is concerned?"

The Marquis shook his head.

He did not reply because, as all his men-friends knew, he never discussed his love-affairs.

At the same time, Charles Toddington understood and was astounded.

It seemed extraordinary that the Marquis should tire so quickly of a Beauty who had been acclaimed as an "Incomparable" from the moment she entered the Social World.

Now, after two years of widowhood, she was at the height of her beauty and pursued by every eligible bachelor in London.

He had in fact been quite certain that his friend the Marquis was "hooked" at last, and had even spent some time trying to decide what he should give him as a wedding-present.

And yet he had felt in the last two days of the house-party which had gone on too long that the Marquis was growing restless and Lady Isme was over-playing her hand.

The daughter of the Duke of Dorset, she had made a very bad marriage for anyone so beautiful, and her father had been hoping for a more important son-in-law than a raffish, unreliable Baronet whose fortunes were as vacillating as his heart.

There is no doubt he would have made Isme, who was far younger than he was, extremely unhappy had he not been killed at Waterloo and thereby conveniently passed out of her life.

Even before the conventional time of mourning was past she had been fêted and acclaimed, and it seemed as if even the bells of London rang with her name and praised her beauty.

When she first saw the Marquis of Heroncourt after he had returned from Wellington's Army back into civilian life, she knew that he was the husband she had always wanted.

He was also exactly the son-in-law her father had desired, his views only to be ignored by his daughter who insisted that she was in love and nothing else was of any consequence.

"I hear you have Heroncourt running after you, Isme,"

he had said to her a month ago.

"There is no secret about that, Papa!"

"It is the best news I have heard for a long time!" the Duke said urgently. "Grab him while you can, and do not make a mess of your life a second time."

There was no need for the Duke to elaborate, for his daughter knew he was referring to the disaster her marriage had undoubtedly been.

She could only thank her lucky stars that Frederick had not returned from the war.

She had been so positive in thinking when he swept her off her feet with his ardent and very experienced love-making that they would be ideally happy.

Only to be disillusioned as only somebody very young could be when they face for the first time the crude facts of life.

Frederick Churton was everything that was undesirable in the permanent relationship of marriage.

He found it impossible to resist a pretty woman, just as he found it impossible not to throw away what little money he had on the most reckless extravagance and without a thought for tomorrow.

He gambled for stakes that were too high, he drank too much, and it was only people who had a very slight acquaintance with him who found his ardent pleasure-seeking amusing and enjoyed his company.

He was flirting with other women even before he and Lady Isme had finished their honeymoon.

She soon found that the poetical eloquence which had been so fascinating when he made love to her rapidly lost its charm when she realised it had been repeated and re-repeated to hundreds of women before her and would continue to be heard again by no fewer in the future.

"How could I have been such a fool?" Lady Isme had asked herself desperately.

When she learned of her husband's death, she did not pretend to her father that it was anything but a welcome release.

"You were right, Papa, and I promise you I will never make another mistake," she said.

There was no question of her making a mistake where the Marquis was concerned.

He was everything she wanted in a husband from the point of view of social position, wealth, and possessions, besides being the most attractive of the *Beaux* who centred around the Prince Regent.

"We shall make a perfect couple," Lady Isme told herself, knowing that while there was always the fear that one might emerge, at the moment there was no Beauty on the horizon to make her afraid she would be toppled from her pedestal.

She was indeed so provocatively beautiful that it seemed extraordinary that the Marquis should have decided in such a short time that he was no longer interested.

Watching him as he walked from the window to stand in front of the fireplace, Charles Toddington thought it was not surprising that women fell into his arms almost before he was aware of them or even asked their names.

It was not only that he was remarkably good-looking, he had an air of consequence about him and what Charles thought was an aura of leadership which made it impossible for anyone, man or woman, to ignore him.

He had been an outstanding Officer in Wellington's Army, receiving two medals for gallantry, and having deserved a dozen more.

The men who served under him had adored him and would have been prepared to march through the gates of Hell, should he have asked it of them.

Although he could, as Charles knew, be hard at times and ruthless in getting his own way, he was always completely just and could be surprisingly compassionate, which somehow seemed at variance with his other qualities.

Aloud Charles said:

"The trouble with you, Drogo, is that you have too much and that leaves you nothing to fight for."

"What do you mean, too much?" the Marquis asked sharply.

"Exactly what I say," Charles replied, "too many personal qualifications, looks, and talents, as well as too many possessions. I doubt if you have even had time to count them all and, where women are concerned, too much damned charm, so that they cannot avoid falling in love with you."

"Shut up, Charles, you are making me feel sick!" the Marquis said. "What you are saying is really nothing to do with what I am feeling at the moment."

"Then what is wrong?" Charles asked simply.

"I can give you the answer to that," the Marquis replied. "I am missing the war! I am missing the tension, the excitement, the fear, if you like, the feeling that one could never relax and be certain that a stray bullet would not knock one for six."

"That is one aspect of war," Charles said, "but you seem to have forgotten the discomfort of sleeping in the open or in some filthy building infested with fleas, going for days without food and finding it when it did arrive to be completely inedible, drinking the local wine, know-

7

ing as one did so that it was so raw as to be poisonous!"

The Marquis laughed.

"I suppose both our pictures are true, but I still say it is the monotony of peace that is making me feel as though I am being suffocated in a goose-feathered bed and only a cold shower could make me breathe again."

Charles did not reply, and after a moment the Marquis said:

"I know you are thinking I am ungrateful and, as you said, I have so many possessions I should be going down on my knees to thank God for them. At the same time I feel half-dead, and I miss the constant planning we had to do in order to keep alive."

"Well, all I can say," Charles Toddington answered, "is that I prefer peacetime soldiering. It may be all 'spit and polish,' and if there is one thing that is boring, it is charging about on a barrack square. But at least I have a comfortable bed to sleep in at night, and there is no need for one to be lonely in it!"

He saw the expression on his friend's face and laughed.

"All right, Drogo," he said, "I know what you are thinking! But you know as well as I do if you are honest, that when we go back to London you will be back on the chase, finding yourself intrigued, fascinated, and finally captivated by a pair of alluring eyes that seem different from any eyes you have seen before."

"That is just the point!" the Marquis said bitterly. "They *do* seem different from anything one has seen before until one takes a second look. then to one's consternation, one finds they are exactly the same! The same old tricks, the same old enticements, the same twist of the lips, touch of the hand, and—Hey, presto!—where does it all lead one?"

"Into bed."

"Exactly!" the Marquis agreed. "Then one finds despairingly there is nothing new, and one is back looking again for a pair of eyes that are 'different.'"

"My God, Drogo, you have got the 'glooms' badly, and no mistake! I can only hope that somebody will challenge you to a duel, or that you will wake up tomorrow morning and find you are bankrupt! That should sweep away your depression!"

"I am being serious, Charles," the Marquis said in a tone of reproach.

His friend laughed.

"Far too serious for me! If you are depressed, so am I!"

"But is there nothing we can do about it?"

"I suggest we take two of your fastest horses and gallop them until they, and we, are exhausted!"

"I suppose there is nothing else we can do," the Marquis said, "and perhaps, after all, it would have been wise to have asked one or two of the party to stay on."

"They would have been only too eager to accept," Charles replied. "And I have no wish to watch you stifling your yawns at dinner, as you did last night, when Quentin was telling his most outrageous stories."

"I have heard them all before!"

"So have I, now I come to think of it," Charles agreed. "So you must be right, Drogo! We must find ourselves a whole collection of new friends whose jokes, tricks, and allurements will be new at least to us."

"For how long?" the Marquis asked.

Charles rose from his chair and stretched his arms.

He was the same height as the Marquis and they were the same age. They had known each other since child-

9

hood and had been close friends at Eton and joined the Household Cavalry on the same day.

To the Marquis, Charles was the brother he never had and to Charles, who was not at all well off, Drogo made all the difference in his life.

A life that was luxurious, glamorous, and amusing.

Although he was taking it lightly and teasing him, Charles was actually perturbed that the Marquis was becoming disillusioned so quickly with life as a country gentleman with large estates, which should have occupied both his time and his mind.

Unfortunately they were so well run for him and so excellently administered, there was really nothing for the Marquis to do.

Although the Regent was constantly demanding his company and there was not a door in London that was not open to him, the Marquis grew quickly more bored in London than he was in the country.

At least here, which was his ancestral home and the most magnificent of the houses he possessed, he had his horses, his dogs, his private race-course, and a dozen more things to occupy his time.

Although Charles had seen the disillusionment and restlessness growing in the Marquis in the last month or so, he had not realised until now how far it had developed.

Now wondering what he could suggest in order to arouse the Marquis's interest while there appeared to be nothing except what he called the monotony of day-to-day activities, he could only say a little more urgently than he had before:

"Go on, Drogo, order your best horses, we must take some exercise."

"I suppose that is the palliative for all ills," the Marquis said sourly. "If you tire yourself out physically, it is too much effort to think."

"Oh, for Heaven's sake!" Charles said. "You know as well as I do that nothing would stop you thinking. What we are trying to find is something to stop you complaining."

The Marquis laughed.

"Now you are making me ashamed of myself, which I am sure you intended. Damn you, Charles, you have always been so infernally cheerful and grateful for small mercies!"

"I do not call being at Heron a small mercy," Charles argued, "and riding your horses is a very large benefit for which I am prepared to express my gratitude very volubly."

The Marquis put out his hand to tug at the bell-pull.

"You are quite right, Charles," he said. "We will ride until we are too tired to think of anything but enjoying an excellent dinner, thankful that we have no one to entertain but ourselves."

He was certainly now feeling more cheerful, Charles thought, and he was quite certain that once they had been riding for several hours, the Marquis would be back to his normal self.

It was unlike him to be so introspective, and yet Charles knew uncomfortably there was some truth in the fact that they both missed the excitement of war and were finding it difficult to adjust to a quiet, uneventful peace.

A servant opened the door.

"Two horses, for Major Toddington and myself," the Marquis said, "and tell Groves I want the fastest we have in the stables."

"Very good, M'Lord," the servant said, "and there's a lady here who wishes to see Your Lordship."

"A lady?"

"Yes, M'Lord. And she's got a young gentleman with her."

The Marquis frowned.

"Callers!" he said to Charles. "We have no wish to be delayed at the moment."

The Marquis turned to the footman.

"Who is the lady? Did she give her name?"

"No, M'Lord, she said you wouldn't know her, but she had to see you on a very important matter."

"Well, order the horses and show the lady in!" the Marquis said.

"Very good, M'Lord."

As the servant shut the door the Marquis added to Charles:

"I have a feeling that the importance of her mission is nothing more than a demand for money for the local Church, or a complaint that my cows have ruined her front garden, or some equally trivial incident."

"Perhaps you will be surprised," Charles said optimistically.

"There is not a chance of that," the Marquis said. "Surprise is something we have left behind us in France, and I bet you a 'fiver' my guess is right and she is either begging or complaining."

"Very well, I will take you!" Charles said. "It is worth risking a fiver to prove you wrong for a change. If you want the truth, I am fed up with your infallibility."

Now the Marquis laughed, and it was a spontaneous sound.

As he did so the door opened and a footman said:

"A lady to see you, M'Lord!"

She came into the room, and to the Marquis's surprise she was very young and very pretty.

His experienced eye told him that her riding-habit was slightly old-fashioned and well worn.

At the same time, it seemed to enhance the freshness of her face, the translucence of her skin, and the gold of her hair.

As she advanced towards him he was aware hers was not the conventional prettiness which was described as "an English rose" and greatly admired in London.

There was about her something far more subtle, almost, he thought to himself, as if she were one of the goddesses who had stepped down from her niche in the Hall.

Walking beside her came a young boy of perhaps ten or eleven years old.

He too was very good-looking, with classical features, and there was a resemblance to the girl which told the Marquis they were undoubtedly brother and sister.

"Good afternoon!" he said as the newcomers reached where he was standing in front of the fireplace. "I am the Marquis of Heroncourt, as I expect you know, but you did not give your name to my servants."

"I did not give it, My Lord," the girl answered in a soft musical voice, "because it has been impossible for my grandfather to call on you. But we are in fact neighbours, and I am Mimosa Field."

There was a pause while the Marquis thought before he said:

"Your grandfather is the Earl of Petersfield?"

"My grandfather is dead, My Lord."

"I am sorry. I was not aware of that."

"There is no reason why you should be, except that we live in the same County. My grandfather has been ill for some years, which is why we have been unable to entertain or welcome you back from the War."

"Will you sit down," the Marquis invited, "and tell me how I can help you? But let me first introduce my friend, Major Charles Toddington."

Charles Toddington bowed and Mimosa dropped him a small curtsy before she said, putting a hand on the shoulder of the boy who stood beside her:

"This is my brother James, who is now on my grandfather's death the Fourth Earl."

She spoke the last words as if there was a special meaning in them.

Then she seated herself in the armchair that the Marquis indicated while her brother took the chair next to hers.

The Marquis was aware that he was looking at him with admiration, and expected that the young boy had heard of his horses and was hoping before he had to go he would have a chance of seeing his stables.

"Now, what can I do for you, Lady Mimosa?" the Marquis asked as Charles also seated himself, leaving him the only one standing.

There was a minute's silence, as if she were feeling for words, then she said in a hesitating little voice:

"You may think it very . . . strange that I have . . . come to you, My Lord, when we are not . . . acquainted . . . and I should have sought the help and advice of other people in . . . the County . . . whom I have known since a child but . . . I had a feeling they . . . would not understand."

"Let me promise you that I am delighted to be of assistance, if it is possible," the Marquis said.

"I feel that for you it is possible," Lady Mimosa answered, "because you have . . . been in the War and have been in danger . . . and you will understand while . . . other people would not."

The Marquis looked puzzled.

"I think you must explain what I am to understand," he said.

He smiled at her in a way that most women found irresistible, knowing she was both shy and nervous, and wondering what on earth she could want of him.

He remembered, now he thought about it, that the Earl of Peterfield's estate, which was not a very large one, lay to the north of his own.

Unless he was mistaken, his father had always said that the Earl farmed his land badly because he had stuck to old methods and the old ideas and was not interested in moving with the times.

Nevertheless, most farms had been profitable during the War and the Marquis thought it was unlikely that the Earl had not managed, as every other landlord had, to produce the food that was so urgently needed.

It was very different now with cheap supplies flooding in from the Continent, and the farmers were finding it difficult to make ends meet.

However, he could not imagine this was the subject about which Lady Mimosa had come to see him, and once again, as if he felt she should be more positive, he said:

"Please explain to me, Lady Mimosa, exactly what it is you require me to do."

She looked down and he realised that her eyelashes were very long against the paleness of her skin.

Then she said:

"I am so afraid . . . that you will . . . laugh at me and say . . . I am being hysterical . . . when I tell you . . . why I have come to you. It is . . . only because I am desperate that I . . . ventured to do so."

There was a note, the Marquis thought, of fear in her voice, and because he wanted to set her at ease he said:

"Before we go any further, may I offer you a little refreshment? A glass of wine, some champagne, if you like. And I am sure your brother would enjoy some lemonade."

There was no mistaking the eager way in which the young boy's eyes responded to the suggestion, and the Marquis walked to the grog-tray in the corner of the room.

He poured out a tumbler of lemonade, and without waiting for Lady Mimosa to reply poured half a glass of champagne from a bottle that had already been opened.

He carried the drinks back to where Lady Mimosa sat very still, her eyes watching him, and he knew without being told that she was apprehensive of what his reaction might be to what she had to tell him.

Because she was behaving so strangely, he began to feel curious as to what she could possibly have to say, and as he put the glass of champagne into her hand he said:

"Drink this. I have a feeling that because you have decided to come here and see me you did not eat very much luncheon before you left."

Her eyelids fluttered and a little colour came into her cheeks as she answered:

"That is . . . true . . . but I do not . . . know how you can be . . . aware of it."

"I am also aware," the Marquis said quietly, "that you are very worried about something, and, as I have already

16

said, I am prepared to help you if it is humanly possible. I cannot believe that any problem cannot be solved if one is intelligent about it."

"That is what I have . . . tried to be," Lady Mimosa said, "but I am so afraid that when I tell you why I have come, you will think I am just . . . hysterical, and fancying things that are . . . definitely untrue."

As she spoke the Marquis realised that the hand with which she was holding the glass of champagne was trembling.

He glanced at Charles Toddington before he said:

"My friend Major Toddington will tell you that I had the reputation when I was serving under Wellington of being perceptive as to whether things were true or false."

He paused before he added:

"As you can imagine, in war we had to deal with thousands of rumours, dubious information, and I was often confronted by lies designed simply to confuse us."

He smiled before he went on.

"I am not boasting when I tell you that quite often, when these things happened, the Duke of Wellington would send for me to ask me if I toasted the informant if I believed the information was accurate. Often I had to take a chance, or rather be brave enough to convince those older and in many ways more experienced than myself that what they were listening to was just fanciful."

As he finished speaking Lady Mimosa drew in her breath and he thought he had reassured her. Then she said:

"I swear to you that what I am saying is not . . . a fancy. I believe it to be . . . completely and absolutely the truth when I . . . tell you that my brother is in . . . danger of being . . . murdered!"

As she finished speaking both the Marquis and Charles

Toddington stared at her in astonishment.

"Murdered?" the Marquis asked after a moment's silence. "What do you mean by that?"

"It seems so . . . terrible when I think of the . . . word," Lady Mimosa said unhappily, "but there is a man who would . . . benefit by his death, who would inherit the title he now holds, and whose only way of becoming the Fifth Earl in succession to my grandfather is for Jimmy to . . . die."

Her voice broke on the last words and her eyes filled with tears as she looked up at the Marquis to say piteously:

"Please . . . please . . . will you save him? I . . . cannot think of anyone except you . . . who could . . . help us."

The Marquis sat down in an armchair beside Lady Mimosa and said quietly:

"Now suppose you start at the beginning and tell me exactly what is happening and why you suspect that your brother's life is in danger?"

Lady Mimosa drew in her breath as if to force herself to be calm, but her hands were shaking as she set the hardly touched glass of champagne down on a small table beside her chair.

Then clasping her fingers together she said:

"My grandfather had a nephew, Norton Field, who is my father's first cousin, and has always coveted the house and the title. Since my grandfather had only one son, Norton Field is now heir presumptive to my . . . brother."

The Marquis was listening intently as Lady Mimosa went on:

"For some reason Cousin Norton did not go to the War and after he left Oxford in a very short time he ran up such large debts in London that his father begged

Grandpapa to pay them, saying that he could not afford to do so."

"And your grandfather paid?" the Marquis asked.

"He was very angry at having to do so, seeing that Norton had no right to be so extravagant, and pointing out that his money was needed to keep up the family house and estates which would eventually go to Jimmy."

"Did you see much of your cousin?" the Marquis enquired.

"He came near us only when he wanted money from Grandpapa, who after a time refused to give him any more. Then one night there was a burglary at the house, and, although I am unable to prove it, I feel certain it was Cousin Norton who had stolen some of the silver and one or two small pictures. All of it we learned later was sold, but they never found the culprit."

She paused, and because he was interested the Marquis said urgently:

"Go on!"

"Then when Grandpapa died quite recently, Cousin Norton, whom I had not seen for a long time, came to the funeral. Afterwards I found him ferreting around the house and inspecting some of the more valuable pieces, almost as if he were appraising them.

"'Everybody has left, Cousin Norton,' I said, 'and as I am very tired, you will understand that I wish to retire to bed.'

"'So you want me to leave, you want to turn me out as my uncle did?' he replied. 'But one day I intend to live here. It is ridiculous to expect a child of James's age to look after everything and be the head of such an il-lustrious family as ours!'

"'Jimmy is young, but he will grow older,' I said,

'and Grandpapa always thought he had the right ideas and would follow very ably in his footsteps.'

"'Grandfather talked a lot of nonsense!' Cousin Norton said rudely. 'The Earl of Petersfield should be a man of at least my age, a man of the world, a man who knows how to keep up the dignity of an ancient family and take his place at Court!'"

Lady Mimosa gave a little shiver as she said:

"There was something . . . unpleasant in the way he spoke . . . something that made me suspect that he wished to be rid of Jimmy and would not hesitate if he got the chance to do so!"

"I can understand your feeling like that," the Marquis said soothingly, "but is there any proof that he has any real criminal intent towards the boy?"

Lady Mimosa was silent, almost as if, the Marquis thought, she were praying she could make him understand. Then she said:

"Cousin Norton went away, and since he has gone some very strange things have happened."

"What sort of things?" the Marquis asked sharply.

"First a great stone crashed from the roof, just missing Jimmy as he was going out to ride a horse that was waiting for him. There was no reason why it should suddenly have become dislodged from its position."

"It missed me by only a few inches!" Jimmy said unexpectedly. "If I had not turned back because I had dropped my whip, it would have hit me on the head and killed me!"

Lady Mimosa made a sound that was almost a sob and put out her hand as if to protect her brother, then replaced it in her lap before she continued:

"Jimmy and I always ride the same way through a

wood to a piece of open and level ground, where we can gallop our horses. It is usually Jimmy who rides ahead. But yesterday morning he overslept and came down to breakfast just as I finished.

"'There is no hurry,' I said. 'I will ride on slowly, and you can catch me up. But promise me you will finish your breakfast.'

"He promised and I went out and mounted my horse which was restless and rode him slowly through the Park into the Wood.

"I was riding along not thinking of anything except the sun coming through the leaves and how beautiful everything looked, when I saw a rabbit running ahead of me down the path, which at that point was quite level.

"Then suddenly to my astonishment I saw it spring high into the air almost like a dog rather than a rabbit!

"It was so strange that I drew in my horse to see why it should have jumped in that strange manner and saw the ground was broken at that particular place."

She made a sound like a groan before she exclaimed:

"By the mercy of God I was curious enough to dismount and walk ahead to look and see what had happened."

Her eyes were wide and frightened as she said:

"It was a man-trap that had recently been laid deep into the path. If Jimmy had ridden up to it quickly, as he would normally have done, being in a hurry to get to the ground where we could gallop, his horse would have been caught in the trap and would have flung him, which might quite easily have broken his neck!"

She paused before she added:

"It was then, when I was so frightened, I decided I must have help. Then last night something woke me."

"What was it?" the Marquis enquired.

"It was a very faint noise, but because it was different from the squeak of a bat or the bark of a fox in the woods I woke up."

"What happened?" the Marquis asked.

"I heard somebody entering the house on the ground floor. It was dark outside and there was no moon, but the stars were very bright, and when I leant out of the window, I could see a man . . . just the outline of him . . . climbing through a window he had managed to unlatch. I was terrified as to who he might be and why he was in the house.

"There was no one I could alert. The servants are all quite old and sleep in a different part of the house from Jimmy and me."

"So what did you do?" the Marquis asked.

"I crept to Jimmy's room, entered it, and locked myself in. He was sound asleep and did not stir. I waited by the locked door as somebody came along the passage outside very, very quietly, making so little sound that they would never have been heard by anyone who was asleep."

"Then what happened?"

"I saw the handle of Jimmy's door turn, but I had locked it, and whoever it was realised it would not open and went away!"

Lady Mimosa finished speaking.

Then with a little gesture of her hands that was very appealing and at the same time pathetic she said in a voice vibrant with fear:

"Help me . . . please help me . . . I do not know . . . what to . . . d-do!"

chapter two

WHILE Lady Mimosa was speaking, the Marquis was staring at her as if he could hardly credit that what she was saying was the truth.

Then as she finished her appeal for help it was as if his mind leapt into action and he took over command of the situation.

Watching him, Charles Toddington thought with a smile that the Marquis had certainly lost his bet and, what was more, he was back in form just as he had been in the War when some particular movement of the enemy gave them a new challenge and a fresh awareness of danger.

"Tell me about your cousin," the Marquis said quietly. "Who is he and what is he like?"

"As I said, a first cousin of my father," Mimosa replied, "who was killed seven years ago in the Peninsula, and Norton is a year younger than he was."

Vaguely the Marquis remembered hearing that a neighbour, the Viscount Field, only son of the Earl of Petersfield, had been killed in action.

"What Regiment was your father in?" he asked.

"The Grenadiers," Mimosa answered, "and we were told he fought very gallantly at the Battle of Torres Vedras."

"I am very sorry that you lost him," the Marquis said.

"My mother never really recovered from it," Mimosa replied. "She gave up our home, which was on the estate, and we went to live in the big house with Grandpapa. But Mama was never the same and three years ago she died. I am convinced that it was from a . . . broken heart."

The way Mimosa spoke was very moving, and for a moment there was silence.

Then the Marquis said gently:

"You were telling me about your cousin."

"Yes . . . of course. As I have already told you, he did not go to war, but spent his time in London, and I think Grandpapa was ashamed of him, besides resenting the way in which he was always badgering him for money."

"I have often seen him at White's!" Charles Toddington interrupted.

The Marquis turned his head to look at his friend.

"You have, Charles? Would I remember him?"

"There is no reason why you whould," Charles replied. "He is a rather unpleasant-looking chap, over-dressed, almost a Dandy in appearance, and associated with the hard-drinking, noisy crowd who make a nuisance of themselves up in the card-room."

The expression on the Marquis's face was very eloquent before he said to Mimosa:

"I can understand your grandfather feeling that his nephew was behaving in a foolhardy manner."

"If only Papa were alive, he could tell you far better than I can what Cousin Norton is like. But I remember his saying that he was very vindictive."

"What did he mean by that?"

"Apparently," Mimosa answered, "when he was at Eton he expected to be chosen to row for his House, and when this did not happen he bored a hole in the boat during the night and plugged it with some substance that dissolved in water. As soon as the boat was launched it sank. Fortunately it was in a shallow part of the river, so that no one was drowned."

The Marquis stared at her as if he could hardly believe what he was being told, then he said:

"Was this known? Was he not punished for it?"

Mimosa shook her head.

"No, but Papa knew, and he said because Cousin Norton got away with it, he used to boast about how clever he had been and how he had paid out those who had prevented him from being one of the crew as he had wanted."

"If he does things like that," the Marquis said dryly, "it makes your story of what has happened now seem much more convincing."

"I was afraid you would not believe me," Mimosa said, "but because you were so brave and successful against the French, I felt that only you would be able to compete with the villainy of Cousin Norton."

Listening, Charles Toddington thought with amusement that the Marquis had had many compliments paid to him, but this was perhaps one he would really appreciate.

The Marquis had been listening intently to everything Mimosa had to tell him and he said only:

"Tell me more."

She made a little gesture with her hands.

"There is really very little more. I have not seen very much of Cousin Norton. In fact, I have avoided him until he came to the funeral, and then . . . to be honest . . . he frightened me!"

"You must try not to be afraid," the Marquis said.

"How can I help it?" she asked. "Jimmy is so young, and the reason why I came to you was that I was sure none of our relatives who live near, even if they believed me, would wish to become involved in anything so unpleasant."

"That I can understand," the Marquis said quietly, "and now we have to decide what is to be done about you both."

Jimmy put down his empty glass and as he did so said:

"I do not want to die. I want to be a soldier, like Papa."

"I am sure that is what your father would want too," the Marquis said, "and he would also want you to be very brave and prevent your sister from being too frightened by what is happening."

"I am not frightened!" Jimmy boasted. Then as he met the Marquis's eye he added: "Well, only a little bit, after the stone from the top of the house fell so near me."

"That is certainly something that must not happen again," the Marquis said. "What I suggest, Lady Mimosa, is that you and Jimmy come to stay here while we consider what can be done about you in the future."

Mimosa's eyes widened in surprise as she said:

"Do you . . . really mean we can . . . stay with you?"

"I think it is taking unnecessary risks for you to be in your own home if, as you tell me, you and Jimmy live alone."

She looked faintly embarrassed before she answered:

"I know that after Grandpapa died I ought to have asked somebody to come to stay with me, but there seemed to be nobody very suitable or who would be pleased to do so, and when things began to happen, I found it difficult to . . . think of anything else."

"Yes, of course," the Marquis said soothingly. "But what I think you should do now is to send a carriage back for your belongings—I presume if you ask for what you want, there will be a maid to pack them for you?"

"Yes, of course," Lady Mimosa agreed.

"Then suppose you sit down at that desk over there," the Marquis suggested, "and write a note to one of your servants while I arrange for a carriage, together with my valet, who will make sure that nothing of importance is overlooked, to go over and pick up whatever you have asked for."

"You are very kind," Mimosa murmured.

"And very efficient!" Charles added, smiling as he spoke. "In fact, you will discover, Lady Mimosa, that the Marquis is at his best when he is organising a campaign, and that is what you have become at this particular moment!"

"I—I hope so," Lady Mimosa said fervently. "At the same time, My Lord, we would not wish to be an encumbrance or . . . a nuisance to you. When I came here, I never thought for a moment that you would . . . ask us to be your . . . guests."

"If I am to believe everything you have told me," the

Marquis said, "we must take every precaution to keep Jimmy safe, and make certain there are no more apparent attempts on his life such as you have already narrated."

"Thank you . . . thank you for being so kind," Mimosa said, "and for not telling me I was making a 'mountain over a mole-hill,' which is what I was afraid . . . you might do."

The Marquis laughed.

"This is certainly something very different," he said, "but I think however serious it sounds, we must try to keep our sense of humour."

"If I am going to stay here with you, My Lord," Jimmy said, obviously following his own train of thought rather than listening to what was being said, "can I ride your horses?"

"Jimmy!" Mimosa said quickly before the Marquis could reply. "That is not something you should ask!"

"But he has the best horses in the whole country!" Jimmy protested. "You said so yourself!"

Mimosa looked at the Marquis apologetically.

"I am sorry," she said, "but Jimmy loves horses, and because Grandfather was so ill for so long, the horses at home have grown old, and there was nobody to agree that we should buy or breed any young ones."

The Marquis realised she was embarrassed and to put her at her ease, he said:

"I can assure you, Lady Mimosa, as my friend Major Toddington and I are here alone, and my stables are full, we should be delighted to have your help and Jimmy's with horses, which in my opinion never have enough exercise."

He saw Mimosa's eyes light up and guessed that she was as excited about riding his horses as her brother was.

Then as Mimosa moved to sit at the desk and write a letter to the Housekeeper at her home, Jimmy said excitedly to the Marquis:

"I want to ride a really fast, spirited horse! It is very frustrating to go slow when one really wants to go fast!"

Charles laughed.

"I agree with you, young man. At the same time, we would not want you to end up with a broken collarbone or a fractured leg just when we have to fight a battle on your behalf!"

Jimmy looked excited.

"Is that what you are going to do?"

"It appears we have little choice," the Marquis said dryly. "I hope, Charles, that you have some original ideas as to how we are to start. The main difficulty, as I see it, is to bring him out into the open."

The eyes of the two men met, and they were both thinking that once Norton Field was aware that the Marquis of Heroncourt was involved, he would be on his guard.

Perhaps for the moment he would make no further movement to eliminate the young boy who stood in his way to the Earldom until the excitement over what had happened had died down and they had reverted to a false sense of security.

"I know what you are thinking, Charles," the Marquis said quietly, "and I am thinking the same thing."

He paused for a moment, then he said:

"I have an idea!"

"What is it?" Charles Toddington asked, and Mimosa raised her head from the letter she was writing to look at him.

"Now I think about it," the Marquis went on, "we

have to have a plausible reason for inviting Lady Mimosa and Jimmy to stay here. If Norton Field thinks they have come here for sanctuary, he will obviously draw in his horns and sit waiting until they are bored when nothing happens, and return home."

"I see what you mean," Charles said. "Then what is your idea?"

The Marquis did not answer him but looked down at Jimmy and said quietly:

"Now, listen to me, young man. This is very serious and it concerns you. As I have just said, we have to have an excuse for having you and your sister here. What I am going to suggest is that you are staying here because you are not well enough to return home, and that is what we must make people believe."

There was silence, then Jimmy asked:

"What are you asking me to do, My Lord?"

"I am suggesting that we all go riding," the Marquis said, "and when you have enjoyed galloping on what I promise you will be a very spirited horse, we will come back, but you will be riding on the front of my saddle and Major Toddington will be leading your horse."

Jimmy looked puzzled, and the Marquis went on to explain:

"You will have had a fall. It will not be serious, but you are slightly concussed. Do you know what the means?"

"Yes, of course," Jimmy answered. "I fell out of a tree last year when I was nearly at the top. When I hit the ground I saw stars and afterwards I had a terrible headache."

"Right!" the Marquis said. "Now you have to be very clever, and when I bring you back here after our ride, you are only half-conscious, your head hurts you badly, and I shall think it is a mistake for you to return home until you have seen a doctor."

The Marquis turned to Mimosa, who was listening intently and said:

"Tear up your letter and start again. Say that Jimmy has had a fall out riding and you are therefore obliged to stay here tonight, and probably longer, until he is very much better. Then ask for what you need and the carriage will bring back your things later in the evening."

"I think that is very clever of you."

Then she gave a little cry.

"You do not think that . . . Cousin Norton will try to injure Jimmy while . . . he is here?"

"If he does, we shall be ready for him," the Marquis said.

He glanced at Charles Toddington as he spoke, and they both knew that was what he was hoping would happen, since he would prefer to fight on his own ground rather than on anybody else's.

"Now," he said, "I am going to order the horses. For the next hour, Jimmy, you can really enjoy yourself. After that, you have to show me that you are not only a good rider, but also a good actor."

"I will try, My Lord."

"You must not make any mistakes!"

"No, of course not," Jimmy said bravely.

"The only person outside this room who will know that you are acting will be my valet. We will be relying on him to nurse you, for as he was with me in the War, he is an expert at any sort of wound or injury."

"It will be exciting being here," Jimmy said, "but it will be rather boring if I have to stay in bed."

"It will not be for long," the Marquis promised. "At the same time, it is absolutely essential that we keep up the excuse for your not returning to your own home and staying with a neighbour who is almost next door."

As if he sensed that Jimmy was disappointed at having to be confined to bed, he said:

"We will have to make sure that despite your injuries you are still capable of enjoying the very delicious dishes which my Chef will provide for you. He is famous for his chocolate pudding which, the Prince Regent complained the last time he came here, made him fatter than he was already!"

Jimmy laughed.

"I love chocolate pudding!"

"Which is something I much enjoyed when I was your age," the Marquis said.

He pulled at the bell, and when the Butler answered it he asked:

"Are the horses ready?"

"Yes, M'Lord. They're waiting outside."

"Then send again to the stables, because Lady Mimosa Field and her brother, the Earl of Petersfield, would like to accompany us. Make sure the horses they ride can keep up with those which Major Toddington and I are riding."

"Very good, M'Lord!"

As the Butler closed the door Mimosa said:

"I am quite certain, My Lord, that we are giving you a great deal of trouble, and that is certainly something I did not intend."

"That may be true," Charles Toddington said before the Marquis could reply, "but I for one am very grateful to you, Lady Mimosa."

"Grateful?"

"Before you arrived my friend was complaining bitterly at the monotony of peacetime England. He was, although I am sure you will not believe me, comparing it unfavourably to the discomforts of the Peninsula!"

"That surely cannot be true!" Lady Mimosa said incredulously.

She looked at the Marquis. Then she said:

"But this is different. There you were fighting an enemy you could see and hear, whereas now it is far more difficult, and might be even more dangerous!"

"I cannot believe that!" the Marquis said lightly.

"On the contrary, I know exactly what Lady Mimosa is saying," Charles said. "It is true that in the Peninsula there was no mistake about whom we were fighting or why. Now our opponent, while suspect, is actually not identifiable, and certainly we have no idea what those who are helping him are like or even if they really exist."

Mimosa drew in her breath.

"It is very . . . very frightening."

"We fought at the Battle of Waterloo," the Marquis said firmly. "And I refuse to be intimidated by sneak-thieves or invisible murderers. If we, intelligent people, cannot match our brains against somebody whom I am convinced is mentally deranged, then I for one will be very ashamed of myself!"

He spoke positively, and Charles knew that he was, in fact, intrigued and even excited by the situation with which he was confronted.

* * *

A little later they rode away from the house, moving under the trees in the Park towards the Marquis's private race-course which was on a flat piece of ground that led down to a twisting stream.

Charles Toddington knew as they went that the Marquis was in a very different mood from the one he had anticipated when he had first suggested they should ride together in order to eradicate his boredom.

Now he was not only talking animatedly to Mimosa, but he had an alert look about him which Charles recognised because it was how he had looked when they were in the Peninsula.

He could never remember a day when they were fighting their way through Portugal and Spain into the south of France when the Marquis had not been full of vitality and verve, encouraging his men and making them laugh even in the most unpleasant situations.

He had evoked in every soldier to whom he spoke a confidence that come Hell or high water, they would be victorious.

"It is the best thing that could have happened to Drogo," he told himself.

He knew that while the Marquis had lost a 'fiver,' what really mattered was that he had been lifted out of the dismal attitude to life to which his house-party had reduced him, into becoming, as Charles described it to himself, a Crusader with a definite aim and object to be achieved.

They went twice round the race-course, the three older members of the group taking the jumps, while Jimmy was instructed to by-pass them.

He was a little disappointed, but the Marquis was taking no chances of his being genuinely injured, seeing that he was riding a horse which was larger, faster, and more difficult to control than anything he had ridden before.

34

But Jimmy was obviously a sportsman, and the Marquis admired not only the way he rode but his eagerness to do anything that anybody asked of him.

Only when they were half-way home did the Marquis lead the way into a small wood.

"Now, Jimmy," he said, "this is where you change your role and show me how well you can act the part of somebody who has just had a very unpleasant and painful fall."

Jimmy gave a little sigh, as if he could hardly bear to give up riding, but he said nothing and obediently dismounted.

Then he patted his horse affectionately on the neck and waited for the Marquis's instructions.

"I suggest first," the latter said, "that you sit down on the mossy ground and get the seat of your breeches dirty."

At first Jimmy looked surprised, then as he understood he grinned and did as he was told.

"Now pick up a little dirt and rub it onto your forehead."

Again Jimmy obeyed him, and Charles said in a low voice to Mimosa, who was watching:

"One thing you will learn about our host is that he has an amazing eye for detail. Nothing escapes him—a soldier's unpolished button, or somebody telling him a lie."

"He is magnificent!" Mimosa said. "And he is more kind than I could ever have expected. At the same time, he is rather frightening!"

Charles raised his eyebrows.

This was not an adjective he had heard to describe the Marquis before.

"Why do you think that?" he enquired.

Mimosa considered the question carefully before she replied:

"He is so . . . authoritative, and the vibrations I feel coming from him seem . . . overwhelming!"

Charles looked even more surprised than he had before.

"I know what you mean," he said, "but . . ."

He paused, then as if she knew what he was thinking, Mimosa said with a smile:

"You did not expect anyone as countrified as me to realise it!"

"That is something I would not say!" Charles protested.

"No, but you thought it."

There was no chance to say any more, for the signal came for Charles to take the bridle of Jimmy's horse.

Then the Marquis lifted the boy onto the saddle in front of him.

"Now lean your head against my shoulder," he ordered, "shut your eyes as if you are either unconscious or in pain, and try to make your body as limp as possible."

"I have to start now?" Jimmy enquired.

He looked through the trees as he spoke and saw that Heron with its fine architectural façade was quite a long way from them.

"You never know who might be watching," the Marquis said, "and we cannot afford, Jimmy, to take any chances. Besides, I think it would be a good idea for you to get yourself into the part you are about to play."

He went on very firmly:

"You must be very convincing when I carry you into the house and up the stairs. And your sister will follow us looking worried and anxious about you."

"I commend you," Charles said mockingly. "I see you have all the art of the Cheltenham Theatricals at your fingertips!"

"Either we do it properly," the Marquis said sharply, "or we send Lady Mimosa and her brother home to face what awaits them there while we wash our hands in a pontifical manner and pretend their problems are not ours."

Lady Mimosa gave a little cry of protest and Charles, smiling, said:

"I stand rebuked! I was, of course, only teasing, Drogo!"

"Quite frankly, Charles," the Marquis said, "I am taking this very seriously."

"How can you be so kind . . . so understanding?" Lady Mimosa murmured. "When I came to see you, I was quite certain you would send me away and tell me I was making a . . . fuss about . . . nothing."

There was a rapt note in her voice that Charles did not miss.

As the Marquis gave her one of his irresistible smiles, he thought that Drogo had made yet another conquest, which was not surprising, although he was doubtful if he would appreciate it.

Compared to lady Isme, Mimosa was very young, very unsophisticated, and undoubtedly countrified.

There was no artifice either in her manner or in her clothes.

She did not disguise her gratitude, nor did she make, Charles noticed, any of the provocative glances or movements that every woman in London affected when the Marquis was present.

Instead, she just looked at him wide-eyed, as a child

might have done, and made no effort to hide her admiration.

'The boy may not lose his life,' Charles thought wryly, 'but his sister will certainly lose her heart!'

At the same time, he was so pleased that the Marquis should be intrigued by the problem which Lady Mimosa had brought him that he was more concerned with what his friend was feeling than with her.

He was, in fact, extremely grateful to her for appearing at exactly the right moment.

Following the Marquis's instructions, Jimmy acted his part extremely well from the moment they drew up outside the front door of Heron.

As a groom came hurrying to the horses' heads and the footmen ran down the steps, the Marquis said sharply:

"His Lordship has had a fall! Send for Henson and Mrs. Dawson!"

Mrs. Dawson was the Housekeeper, and a footman immediately ran up the steps and into the house to find her.

By the time the Marquis had lifted Jimmy very carefully down from the saddle and had carried him into the Hall and had started up the Grand Staircase, Mrs. Dawson, in rustling black silk with a silver chatelaine at her waist, was waiting on the landing.

"The Earl of Petersfield has had a rather nasty fall out riding, Mrs. Dawson," the Marquis said. "I suspect he has slight concussion, and should be put to bed."

"Yes, of course, M'Lord," Mrs. Dawson agreed. "He should be put in the 'Stuart Room.'"

The Marquis thought for a moment, then he said:

"I think the 'Charles II Suite' would be better."

"Very good, M'Lord," Mrs. Dawson agreed. "As I

understand it, a room will also be required for the young lady."

"Lady Mimosa will, of course, wish to stay by her brother," the Marquis said briefly as they walked a little way down the corridor to the Charles II Suite.

It was very impressive and very attractive, with a riot of cupids hovering on the ceiling, carrying a Royal crown in their hands.

The carved and gilt bed, the mirrors, and the furniture were also all embellished with the crown.

Jimmy's room was a little smaller than the one to be used by Mimosa.

There was a *Boudoir* adjoining them both.

It was very much grander than anything Mimosa had ever seen before.

She thought of the rather dull furnishings at her grandfather's house and how exciting it was to be staying with somebody as important as the Marquis.

His possessions were, she knew, admired and envied by everybody who had ever seen them.

After they had left the apparently unconscious Jimmy to be undressed by Henson and put between the sheets, Mimosa sat in the *Boudoir* beside the Marquis and said in a low voice that could not be overheard by the servants:

"Your house is magnificent and it is exactly right for you."

The Marquis looked amused.

"What do you mean by that?" he asked.

Mimosa glanced round the Sitting-Room with its gilded Charles II furniture and high-backed tapestry-covered chairs before she said:

"I can understand that you expect perfection and therefore you achieve it!"

"I think you are flattering me, Lady Mimosa," the Marquis said. "At the same time, I enjoy it and, it is true, I do want perfection, but it is something, unfortunately, that is often out of reach."

"Not where you are concerned," Mimosa said quickly.

She did not look at him as she spoke, and he had the feeling she was not thinking of him as a man but more as something impersonal and godlike, who could make such things possible.

It was such an unusual way for him to be looked at by a young woman that for a moment he thought he must be imagining what she was thinking.

Then he was aware that strangely enough he could read her thoughts.

He supposed it was because she was so simple and unaffected.

And yet he told himself it was something he had never achieved before unless as so often happened, the thoughts of the lady in question had been so banal, so ordinary and, worse still, suggesting the dreaded word *monotonous* that it was impossible for him not to be fully aware of them.

Aloud he said:

"I have put you here, Lady Mimosa, for two reasons: first because I know you will appreciate these particular rooms, and secondly because they are near to mine."

Her eyes turned to his enquiringly, and he explained:

"I am only a short way down the corridor. If by any chance you are disturbed, as you were last night, or afraid of any sort of danger, you must come to me at once. Do you understand?"

She nodded, and he knew that for a moment what he had said was such a relief that she could not find words to express it.

Then she said in a low voice:

"Thank you! Thank you very . . . very much. There is nothing . . . else I can say at the moment."

"Do not thank me yet," he said. "We have a long way to go before we can be sure that Jimmy is safe."

As he spoke he saw the fear come back into Mimosa's eyes.

Then as if she realised that because he was there nothing was so frightening as it had been before, she merely said:

"I—I knew you were the . . . only person who could help . . . us."

chapter three

WHEN Mimosa was dressed for dinner she went first to Jimmy's room to see if he was all right.

He was sitting up in bed eating what she thought was a large supper, including a dish filled with the chocolate pudding which the Marquis had said he had enjoyed as a boy.

Jimmy grinned when he saw his sister and said:

"Ripping food! Far better than we get at home!"

Mimosa looked anxiously towards the door.

"Be careful!" she warned in a low tone. "You are supposed to be suffering from concussion!"

"That is all right," Jimmy replied. "Henson, His Lordship's valet, has told me to eat anything I want and he will say downstairs that as I was not hungry, he finished my dinner for me."

Mimosa laughed.

She knew Jimmy's little ways of always getting what he wanted.

"I will come to see you after dinner," she promised, "and then you should try to go to sleep early. I am sure there will be lots of exciting things to talk about tomorrow."

She did not add that she was tired, having stayed awake all the night before, not only terrified by what had happened, but also turning over and over in her mind to whom she could turn for help.

She was not quite certain why the Marquis had occurred to her and how she was sure he was exactly the person she needed.

It was almost as if she saw him, as she had done once or twice in the past, taking a fence out hunting or riding in a Steeple-chase.

He had been young in those days, and she had been merely a child, and yet she had remembered him.

The last time she had seen him had been five years ago, shortly before he had left for Portugal.

And yet clearly, almost as if he were a picture in a book, she had seen him in front of her eyes, and it was as if somebody told her that he could save Jimmy.

It all seemed extraordinary and even more incredible that she was now a guest in his house, and she was sure that whatever ghastly plots her cousin Norton Field was concocting, the Marquis would defeat him.

She had been told by Mrs. Dawson that they were to meet in the Blue Drawing-Room before dinner.

This was a room she had not yet seen, and when she

was shown into it by a footman she felt as if she were stepping into a dream.

Never had she imagined that a room could be so lovely, with its blue brocade walls, huge chandeliers, and a profusion of Sèvres china, whose blue matched the covering of the carved and gilt furniture.

After a quick glance she had eyes only for the Marquis and Charles Toddington, who were standing at the far end of the room, each with a glass of champagne in his hand.

As she walked towards them she was very conscious of how resplendent they both looked in their evening-clothes, and how dowdy she must look in comparison.

There was another reason also to make her eyes look worried, and it had followed her down the stairs and into the Blue Drawing-Room.

As she dropped the Marquis a graceful curtsy she said:

"I am afraid, My Lord, I have some explaining to do, and I hope you will not think it very intrusive of me to have . . . my dog with . . . me."

The Marquis had already noticed the small, attractive brown and white spaniel that had come with her into the room.

He smiled, then held out his hand to the dog, saying dryly:

"Another unexpected guest!"

"If you insist, I will send him back," Mimosa said quickly, "but your valet told me that when he arrived to collect our luggage, the servants said that Hunter was in such a state because I was not there, that they were afraid he would run away to look for me."

"So his name is Hunter!" the Marquis remarked.

"Jimmy christened him that because he was always

hunting for something, and it is certainly true that he might have run away to hunt for me, and got lost."

The Marquis knew from the way Mimosa was speaking that it was another plea for him to understand and to accept her dog.

To put her at her ease, he smiled and said:

"As I can understand Hunter's devotion to you, I am very pleased for him to stay here as long as he behaves himself."

"Thank you!" Mimosa cried. "I promise you he will be very, very good. He always does as I tell him."

Hunter was licking the Marquis's hand and wagging his tail as if he understood that he had been accepted.

Then the Marquis said:

"Now I will get you a glass of champagne, Lady Mimosa, and I think we should all drink to the success of our campaign against what I am beginning to think may be a very formidable enemy."

"I cannot believe he is worse than Napoleon!" Charles teased. "After all, although it took time, we defeated him in the end."

"I think in these circumstances the one thing we have not got is time," the Marquis remarked.

He passed a glass of champagne to Mimosa, and as she took it from him he said:

"I cannot contemplate weeks, let alone months, of you looking as worried as you do now. You must trust me and believe that you were right in coming to me for help."

"I am quite, quite sure of that," Mimosa said quickly, "but I cannot help worrying, not only about Jimmy, but because we are being a problem to you."

"As I have already told you, that is a very good thing!"

45

Charles interposed. "You have given us something new to think about, Lady Mimosa, besides cabbages and turnips, and I for one am very grateful!"

Mimosa understood that he was deliberately talking lightly, and she forced a smile to her lips and took a sip of champagne before she said:

"I cannot believe anybody could be as lucky as I am to have two such fearless Knights ready to destroy the dragon."

Charles laughed and said:

"Nothing could describe Drogo better. He has always been a Knight Errant, looking for a maiden in distress, and now he has found one!"

"You are letting your imagination run away with you, Charles," the Marquis remarked.

At the same time he was smiling.

He refilled his friend's glass, and as he did so Mimosa said:

"It is very exciting for me to be here at Heron, which I have always been told is very beautiful. But I am afraid you will think it is very unconventional for me not to be in mourning considering that my grandfather has only recently died."

She looked down at her simple muslin gown which the Marquis recognised as being made of a cheap material that no Lady with whom he was acquainted would have condescended to wear.

But on Mimosa, because it was so plain, due to the fact that it was fashionable since the war for gowns to be decorated only round the hem and bodice, it made her look very child-like.

The worried look, however, was back in her large eyes as she explained:

"There has been little time since the funeral for me to go shopping, especially as I have been so perturbed over what was happening to Jimmy."

"Charles and I understand," the Marquis replied soothingly, "and personally I have always abominated the gloom of mourning, which seems completely out of keeping with the message of Christianity, which is, of course, a belief in the Resurrection."

He spoke in the controversial tone which he used when he and Charles were arguing over abstract subjects that were not of any interest to their brother officers.

Then to his surprise Mimosa replied quickly:

"I am so glad that you feel like that. It is what I have always thought myself, and so did Mama. She always said that mourning was wrong because there was no death for those who had died and we were crying for ourselves and not for them."

She paused, then she said in a low voice almost as if she spoke to herself:

"That was why she was eager to be with Papa."

The Marquis's eyes were on Mimosa's face, as if he were taking part in a conversation he had never expected to have with a woman as young as Mimosa.

He could not remember such a thing arising with any of the sophisticated Beauties with whom he spent his time in London.

Aloud he said:

"As you live in the country and we have so much to do in the next few weeks, and I think it unlikely we shall be entertaining in any way, I should just dress as you wish, and forget the conventions which are always extremely boring, and as you have just said often unsuitable."

47

Mimosa's eyes lit up. Then as she looked at him she said:

"I might have guessed you would think like that! And yet I suppose I always knew you would be original in what you thought as well as in what you did."

Once again Charles thought as he listened that she was complimenting the Marquis in a different way from what he might have expected.

He also noticed that Mimosa's appraisement of him was somehow quite impersonal and expressed in the same way that she would have admired a fine picture or piece of furniture in the house.

Now for the moment the worry had gone from her eyes and she smiled as a child might have done as she said ingenuously:

"Now I no longer feel embarrassed as I did when I came down the stairs, worried not only because I had to introduce Hunter to you, but also in case you thought I did not know how to behave properly."

The Marquis laughed.

"I think you behave impeccably, Lady Mimosa, and so, I might add, does Hunter!"

The Marquis looked, as he spoke, at the spaniel who was sitting at Mimosa's feet, his eyes looking from one to the other of the people standing round him almost as if he were listening to what they were saying.

"Hunter and I are very grateful for those kind words, My Lord," Mimosa replied.

For a moment her hand rested on her dog's head.

They went in to dinner and to the Marquis's surprise he found himself embroiled in a serious and extremely interesting conversation on the conventions of different religions and the attitude they held to death.

It ranged from the Pharaohs of Egypt, who were buried with their possessions and even their servants so that they should be comfortable in the next world, to *suttee,* whereby Hindu windows threw themselves on their husband's pyres.

To both men's surprise, Mimosa was able to take part in the conversation in a way which told them she was very well read and extremely knowledgeable on subjects of which most women were completely ignorant.

It seemed extraordinary that a young girl who had lived her life in the country and had not had the advantage of many highly qualified teachers should know so much.

After they had moved from the conventions concerning death to the strange religions to be found in Africa and other undeveloped parts of the world, the Marquis asked Mimosa:

"How can it be possible, Lady Mimosa, that you should know so much about subjects which are certainly not appreciated by other members of your sex?"

Mimosa looked surprised.

"Is that true?" she asked. "I have found them fascinating, but then, I have always wanted to travel as Papa did when he was a young man, being fortunate enough to go with his Regiment to India and to other places in the East, but I have had to travel in my mind."

"I suppose what you are actually telling me is that you have travelled through the books you have read," the Marquis said.

"Exactly!" Mimosa agreed. "Grandpapa had a very large and comprehensive Library, although I am sure not as big as you have here. It included a great number of books about other countries because my great-grandfather was in his way an explorer."

"I thought young ladies read only novelettes," Charles teased.

"I have read some," Mimosa replied, "but I find them very dull compared to accounts of a European disguised as a pilgrim who managed to sneak into Mecca knowing he was in danger of losing his life, or of another man who visited Tibet and saw the Dali Lama."

This meant they were all talking again about the strange hidden places in the world which it was impossible for anybody to visit except in disguise.

They inevitably had a fascination for those who longed to seek the unknown and to explore the secrets that were strictly forbidden to any outsider.

"That is what we ought to be doing, Charles," the Marquis said, "instead of boring ourselves with the commonplace."

Mimosa clasped her hands together.

"I am sure you could find a way to get to Mecca if you wished to," she said, "and be present at the dance of the Dervishes, but the only proper reason for doing so would be to enable you to write a book about them for those less fortunate."

"I thought there would be a snag!" the Marquis exclaimed. "If there is one thing I have no wish to do, it is to write a book!"

"Why not?" Mimosa asked. "Think how much the people who stayed at home would appreciate your personal report on what happened at Waterloo, or at the other battles in which you took part—Vittoria, for instance."

The Marquis looked at her in surprise.

"Who told you I was at Vittoria?" he asked.

"Your valet was telling Jimmy and me how brave you were and how you saved several men's lives by bringing them back to your lines after dark."

The Marquis looked embarrassed.

"Henson should keep his mouth shut," he said, "and I shall tell him so."

"If you do that, it will be very unkind," Mimosa said. "Jimmy had asked him about the battles in which you fought, and because he knew how interested we were he told us what we wanted to know."

She looked worried and said:

"Please . . . I would not wish to get him into . . . any trouble."

The Marquis smiled.

"I promise you he will not do that. Henson is a law unto himself, which you will soon discover if you stay here long enough. I do not suppose I could stop him talking if I tried!"

"If you refuse to write a book," Charles said, "perhaps Henson should do it for you."

They all laughed at this, and the Marquis thought that unexpectedly he had found dinner an amusing meal and very different from what he had anticipated.

When Mimosa, who was by now very tired, excused herself and retired to bed, the two friends were left alone and the Marquis said:

"I expect you have remembered that I owe you a fiver!"

"Of course," Charles replied, "and I am expecting you to pay up, but I had no idea that I was betting on a certainty."

"It seems extraordinary," the Marquis said, "that out of the blue, just when I was complaining about the boredom and monotony of the countryside, this should happen."

"I was thinking about it at dinner," Charles answered,

"and I would never have imagined, and most certainly would have betted against finding a young girl as intelligent as Lady Mimosa!"

"She is certainly original," the Marquis remarked, "and far too young, little more than a child, for this sort of thing."

There was silence. Then he added as if he spoke to himself:

"I suppose it really is true and she has not imagined the whole drama?"

"I might have thought so," Charles replied, "if I had not actually seen Norton Field and also remembered some of his unpleasant habits which I would not mention in front of his cousin."

"What are they?" the Marquis asked.

"Well, for one thing," Charles replied, "he frequents the type of House of Pleasure of which you and I would not cross the threshold!"

The Marquis raised his eyebrows and Charles continued:

"You know the ones I mean, which cater for exotic types of vice which we both find abominable."

The Marquis nodded.

"Apart from that, I remember hearing that he encourages the younger members of the Club when they first join to drink too much, then to gamble, with him, of course, for high stakes, and he is inevitably the winner!"

"If you can prove that," the Marquis said angrily, "I will have him thrown out of the Club. It is the sort of behaviour that should not be tolerated at White's!"

"It is difficult to prevent or to prove," Charles said, "but I am certain I am right in thinking that Norton Field is a very unpleasant character, and it does not surprise me that he has made up his mind to succeed to his uncle's place."

"Do you really think he would go so far as murdering little Jimmy in order to do so?" the Marquis asked.

"I think you will find he is too devious to kill him in an obvious manner, such as shooting him, which he could quite easily do at any time. He might try drowning him, but only if it could be made to look like an accident."

The Marquis was silent before he said:

"I see what you mean, Charles. He is being quite subtle: A stone falling off the roof might happen to anybody; a man-trap is set for animals, not for human beings. But why should he, if indeed it was Norton Field, go to the child's room the other night?"

"I should imagine he intended to kidnap him!"

The Marquis sat up in his chair.

"That never struck me! I was thinking perhaps he intended to strangle him while he slept or smother him with the pillows until he stopped breathing."

"I am quite certain," Charles interposed, "that Norton Field is too clever to do anything that might cast suspicion on him personally, which would prevent him, as he plans, from becoming the Fifth Earl."

He paused as if thinking it out before he went on:

"An incriminating corpse is very difficult to explain away. When somebody disappears, there is always the supposition that they may have run away, and, when eventually they are found dead, then it can always be attributed to their being lost on the moors, or accidentally knocked down in a thick fog, or freezing to death in a snowstorm."

"You have certainly thought it out in detail," the Marquis said.

"I think that is what we have to do," Charles replied. "I do not believe for one moment that Norton Field will come bursting in upon us brandishing pistols or swords. It would make it justifiable for you to shoot him in self-defence, or in an effort to protect Jimmy."

"I agree," the Marquis murmured.

"He will be far more subtle," Charles said, and that is where we will have to start thinking along quite different lines from the way you tackled an enemy in the past who at least wore a uniform by which you could identify him."

"Dammit all!" the Marquis exclaimed. "You are making it sound amazingly difficult."

He rose as he spoke to stand in front of the mantelpiece.

"I cannot believe," he said, "that it is impossible for me to protect one boy from the grasping, murderous clutches of a man who covets his title."

"That sounds very nice on the surface," Charles replied, "but are you really prepared to guard young Jimmy twenty-four hours round the clock for months, perhaps for years, on end?"

"No, of course not!" the Marquis answered. "We have already discussed that, and we have to force Norton Field out into the open."

"That is agreed, but how?" Charles asked. "And how can we guess, or rather, how can you guess how his twisted and, as you quite frankly said, deranged mind will work? What will he do to destroy the boy by some means which will make it impossible for anyone to accuse him of murder?"

The Marquis walked across the room and back before he answered. Then he said:

"I am going to sleep on this, Charles, and in the

morning we will put our heads together as we used to do in Spain and Portugal. We must think how we would act if it were we who were outside this house while our objective, the boy, was inside."

Charles smiled.

"That is a problem which should keep you awake for a few hours tonight. I shall be very surprised, however, if you come up with anything very constructive by breakfast-time."

"I will take a bet with you on that," the Marquis said. "I will think of something that will act as a bait to Norton Field, even if it means I have a completely sleepless night!"

"Very well," Charles said. "I will take you, but first you have to pay me the money I am already owed."

The Marquis laughed.

"You are determined not to let me forget those five golden sovereigns," he said, "but I assure you, Charles, I am not a defaulter!"

"I will make sure of that!" Charles said, and they were both laughing as they went up the stairs.

At the same time, when he went to his room Charles Toddington was thinking how one young girl had managed, by appearing at exactly the right moment, to change the Marquis from a gloomy, dissatisfied, restless young man into someone who was, to put it simply, very much alive.

* * *

As Charles predicted, the Marquis found himself unable to sleep and lay, staring blindly into the darkness, thinking out first one plan, then another.

He was far too intelligent not to realise that it was going to be very difficult.

He knew Charles was right when he said that Norton Field was not going to do anything that was obvious or so dangerous from his point of view as to kill Jimmy by any ordinary means.

It was quite possible, however many men guarded him, to prevent the boy from being shot down in the open, but for Norton Field to be in the vicinity when that happened would, he knew, result in a number of people accusing him, whether they could prove it or not, of murder.

"What can we do? What the devil can we do?" the Marquis asked.

If it was a question of the child being kidnapped, that, he supposed, might have been comparatively easy in his grandfather's house, which he gathered from Henson when he questioned him while he was dressing for dinner was a large rambling building.

A number of ancient servants slept in one wing while the centre block was occupied by the family when they were there.

There had been until tonight only Lady Mimosa and Jimmy in a house which was very easy to break into, and if, as Mimosa had feared, Norton Field had managed to spirit the boy away, it was doubtful if there would have been any chance of his being caught.

The Marquis thought that having abducted him, he would then have taken him miles away from his home, perhaps to the north, perhaps to the south.

It might have been several months later before the boy's body would be found in some ditch.

There would be nothing to connect his death with his cousin, Norton Field, who in the meantime would have been seen in London, at his Club and associating with his disreputable friends.

'That is something I must not allow to happen,' the Marquis thought.

He decided that tomorrow he would move Jimmy even nearer to him than he was at the moment.

Perhaps it would be best for the boy to sleep in a dressing-room that was part of the Master Suite.

As it was, on the second floor it would be impossible for Norton Field to approach him from a window, and if he was in the next-door room, the Marquis, being a very light sleeper, would hear the slightest movement or the opening of a door.

"That is what I will do," he decided.

Then because the night was passing, he forced himself to try to sleep and for a moment to forget Jimmy.

*   *   *

The Marquis was awakened by Henson coming hastily into his room and pulling back the curtains in a noisy manner which was very unlike his usual quiet movements.

As he did so, he said:

"M'Lord! Are you awake, M'Lord?"

The Marquis sat up in bed.

"What has happened?"

He knew before the man spoke that it was something serious and, in fact, he almost anticipated the answer.

"'Is young Lordship's gone—disappeared, M'Lord!"

"What do you mean—disappeared?" the Marquis asked.

"The 'ouse was broken into last night by the door in the Inner Courtyard."

57

The Marquis stared at his valet in disbelief.

The Inner Courtyard was part of the old house which had been left untouched when the rest of the building had been restored and practically rebuilt at the beginning of the last century by his grandfather.

The rooms round the Inner Courtyard were small and were used mostly for storage, although there was an office for his secretary which, of course, was closed at night.

"Tell me exactly what has happened!" the Marquis said, getting out of bed.

"The lock 'ad been drilled away, M'Lord, in a quite expert fashion, an' it's doubtful if we'd ever 'ave known until much later in the day that somebody had broken in in such a manner if it hadn't been for 'Er Ladyship's dog."

"Her Ladyship's dog?" the Marquis repeated. "How does he come into it?"

"I hears 'im whining an' scratching at the door, M'Lord, when I comes along the corridor early to see if His young Lordship wants anything. I expects 'im to be awake although it wasn't yet seven o'clock. But when I peeps in through the door, 'e isn't there!"

"I cannot believe it," the Marquis said beneath his breath.

But he did not interrupt as Henson went on:

"It was then I 'ears the dog whining' and scratchin' next door, an' when I looks in, I finds 'Er Ladyship's gone as well!"

Now the Marquis was dressing himself, and while they were still talking, Henson brought his clothes for him from the wardrobe.

"When I opens the door, M'Lord," the valet went on, "the dog shot past me into the passage and with 'is nose down starts to run until 'e reaches the backstairs.

I follows him, thinkin' as 'ow he might lead me to 'Er Ladyship, and 'e goes twisting round the corridors until, to my surprise, he reaches the door in the Inner Courtyard."

The Marquis was by now pulling on his riding breeches, then he walked to the dressing-table and opened a drawer of it to find a cravat to tie round his neck.

"The door was closed, M'Lord," Henson continued, "but I sees at once that the lock's been bored away."

"What did you do then?" the Marquis asked.

"The dog wanted to go outside, M'Lord, but I thought it would be a mistake to let him out and lose him in case he went searchin' for 'Er Ladyship. I dragged 'im back with me and shut 'im up in her bedroom, where he's barkin' the place down!"

"Quite right, Henson," the Marquis approved, "that was very intelligent of you. I feel the dog will be our only hope of finding out where Her Ladyship and her brother have been taken."

His voice was hard with anger as he told himself it was his fault this had happened and he should have thought of it sooner.

Then he said sharply:

"Go and wake Major Toddington and tell him to get dressed quickly. Tell him I have gone to the stables to order the horses."

Knowing he had received an order that had to be obeyed immediately, Henson disappeared and the Marquis put on his riding-boots without his valet's help.

He shrugged himself into a riding-jacket and would have left the room. But as he reached the passage he turned back and, opening a drawer of a table by his bed, took out a pistol.

The drawer also contained a dog's lead, which he used for his own dogs, and carrying it in his hand, he went down the passage to Mimosa's room.

He could hear Hunter whining and scratching as he did so, and as he opened the door it was with difficulty that he prevented the dog from pushing past him, obviously desperate to find his mistress.

Having attached the lead to Hunter's collar, he looked at Mimosa's bed.

The first thing he noticed was that it was very tumbled, the second was he was almost sure a blanket had been pulled off it, which would account for the extremely untidy state in which the rest of the bed-clothes had been left.

As if to confirm what he was thinking, he walked into Jimmy's room next door and found his bed in exactly the same condition.

It was obvious that the kidnappers had entered the room and gagged and bound their victims before they could properly awake, then, wrapping them in blankets because they were wearing only their nightclothes, had carried them away.

It seemed incredible, absolutely incredible, that this should have happened in his own house while he was sleeping only a few doors away.

Now he knew he was up against a far more wily adversary than he had previously imagined.

Although he would never have admitted it, the Marquis was for the moment not so confident of his own infallibility as he had been in the past.

*   *   *

Mimosa had been deeply asleep and, she thought later, dreaming of the Marquis when she awoke with a stifled scream because a hand was placed over her mouth.

For a moment she could hardly believe it was happening.

Then as her whole body felt the shock that had first frozen her into immobility, she felt a gag pressed into her mouth and she was turned over with her face in the pillow so that it was difficult to breathe while it was tied tightly behind her head.

A rope also encircled her body over her thin nightgown and her hands were pulled back behind her, then the ends of the rope tied her wrists together.

While this was happening somebody was tying her feet together.

It seemed impossible this was actually happening, and as the horror of it seeped through her, she tried to scream but found it difficult enough to breathe, let alone make a sound.

Then she was turned so that she lay on her back, and now she could see by the light of a very small lantern the outline of two dark figures.

They were masked and were very indistinct owing to the fact that they held the lantern close to her as they inspected first her gag, then the ropes around her body, before they pulled a blanket off the bed and enveloped her completely in it.

She could not see either as the two men picked her up in their arms and carried her away.

As they did so she was aware that Hunter was snarling ferociously at them, but they paid no attention except occasionally to kick out at him savagely so that he yelped with pain.

Then as they carried her out of the room she realised as they shut the door they had left Hunter inside, and she could hear him scratching to get out and whining at being left behind.

Then she was being carried swiftly away, and what was terrifying was that the men moved so silently that she could barely hear their footsteps.

In the darkness she felt as if it were almost as if she was dead and being carried from this world into a far more sinister one.

Then they were going down the stairs, and feeling the blood going to her head, she thought it at least prevented her from fainting.

Not a word was spoken, but she knew they must have reached the ground level and were outside because now there was just a faint sound of their footsteps which had not been there before.

She had the feeling they were either wearing slippers or had wrapped some material over their shoes to deaden any sound.

They carried Mimosa for a short distance before she felt herself being lifted into what she thought must be some kind of vehicle and laid down on the floor.

Then there was the sound of a door being softly closed and a moment later there were wheels turning beneath her and she knew that horses, two of them, were pulling her away, although where she was going she had no idea.

She lay still, feeling shocked and extremely uncomfortable with her hands tied behind her and enveloped in the blanket.

They drove on and on, the wheels beneath her rumbling over rough roads, then smoother ones, the horses moving at an unusually quick pace considering they were pulling what she thought now must be quite a heavy carriage.

Finally, when they had been going for what seemed a long time, she moved her head first one way then the other until the blanket which covered her fell open and she found it easier to breathe.

She could still see nothing but darkness, except that high up, and it seemed strange, there was just a faint glimmer of light which she thought must be coming from the window or perhaps a grating of some sort.

She looked at it for some time, then to her relief it became stronger, and she realised the dawn was breaking. A little while later she could see that what she had thought was a window was in fact an open grating through which the light percolated between iron bars.

It was then she turned her head farther round and with a leap of her heart, she saw, although it was indistinct, that she was not alone in whatever was carrying her, but there was another bundle a foot or so away from her, and she knew it must be Jimmy.

chapter four

THE ground beneath the wheels grew more and more rough, and now they were bumping as if there were deep ruts on the road on which they were travelling.

Occasionally the wheels seemed to go over something large and heavy like a stone or a piece of wood.

When this happened, Mimosa was thrown from side to side and finally after one particular lurch she found herself against Jimmy.

Like her, he had managed to move the blanket off his face so that now in the light that was growing brighter through the grating overhead she could see his eyes, dark and afraid.

She longed to say something to comfort him, but she

was in fact as terrified as he was, knowing they had been kidnapped, and by whom.

They were still travelling over very bumpy ground, at the same time going slower and slower, and now there was the swish of what sounded like branches of trees against the sides of the vehicle.

There was also the occasional crunch, as if they had hit something very heavy.

It was difficult to think clearly because she was so frightened, but Mimosa tried to reason to herself where they might be going and what was happening.

She found it impossible, however, to have any clear idea of where she and Jimmy were being taken.

Then as the light overhead increased a little, she realised, and thought she might have guessed it sooner, that they were in a horse-box.

These were used by every owner of a racing-stable in order to convey horses from one race-course to another or from the Saleroom to their home.

Suddenly the wheels stopped turning and there was the sound of movement, although what was happening Mimosa could not imagine.

What made it so eerie was that there were no voices, no one giving orders, and yet things were happening.

She felt herself jump as something was thrown heavily on the roof above them and was followed by another crash and a bump.

Some dust from between the wooden planks came floating down on her and Jimmy.

The daylight that had made the inside of their prison a little lighter was now almost obscured by what she thought were trees, although she could not be sure from the angle at which she was lying.

If it was trees, this meant they were in a wood of some sort, but why? For what purpose?

If they had been kidnapped, surely by this time they would have reached whatever hiding-place Norton Field had chosen for them, and the vehicle that had brought them from Heron would have been abandoned.

Mimosa had a sudden longing for the Marquis, with his clear, concise voice planning what they should do, giving orders and knowing they would be obeyed.

Instead, gagged and bound, she felt not only utterly helpless but also humiliated, and she knew Jimmy would be feeling the same.

Now there were more bumps on the roof and crashes against the sides of the horse-box as if something were being piled against them. She thought too that trees were being felled, but she could not be sure.

With a sudden terror Mimosa wondered if, in fact, having brought them to some spooky place, Norton Field intended to set them on fire.

Then as she wanted to scream and go on screaming, one door of the horse-box opened and there was light.

But almost before she could look or see anything, two men climbed into the box.

She just had a quick glimpse of a face, covered except for two round eyes, before she was turned roughly over to lie on her face as she had on the bed when they gagged and bound her.

She wondered what was about to happen.

Then to her astonishment she felt the rope around her legs being loosened, then the one around her body.

Her hands were left tied, but she was aware that the rope that had encircled her wrists had been cut with a knife from the rope that had encircled her.

She tried to understand what was happening, then as she was left with only the gag over her mouth, she felt the man who had been removing the rope run his hand down the one side of her body.

It was a caress, and she was suddenly afraid now in a different way, and she stiffened as he touched her first on one side, then on the other.

Then his hands were reluctantly to the back of her head, where the gag was tied in place, and as he touched it he spoke.

Because there had been only silence until then, his voice was terrifying.

"I'm taking off your gag," he said, "but if you scream or make one sound for at least an hour after we've left, I swear we will come back to kill you both. Do you understand?"

It was impossible to answer because he had not yet taken the gag from Mimosa's mouth.

He must have realised that she acquiesced, however, for he then undid the knot at the back of her head and pulled the handkerchief roughly from the front of her face.

As he did so he moved swiftly, and she could see another man moving with him out of the vehicle, and the door slammed behind them.

There was the sound of a heavy bar being dropped into place, then footsteps moving over twigs that snapped as they did so before faintly Mimosa could hear the sounds of horses moving away.

She listened, still straining to hear if they had really gone, then Jimmy whispered:

"What has happened? Where are we?"

She turned her face round to look at him, then with

difficulty because her hands were tied she managed to sit up.

"I think it is all right to speak," she said, "as I heard the horses leaving. But we must not scream. They might have left someone on guard."

"Why have we been brought here?" Jimmy asked. "And what is this strange carriage we are in?"

"It is a horse-box," Mimosa said.

She looked around at the wooden walls of it as she spoke. She could see it was very old and she somehow thought it had not been in use for a long time.

In fact, the horse-boxes she had seen recently and even the ones her grandfather used were all of a different design from the one they were in.

Feeling she must be practical, Mimosa said:

"They have left us free except for our hands, and I think, Jimmy, if we sit back-to-back, I will be able to release you, then you can do the same for me."

"Yes, of course," Jimmy agreed.

They did as Mimosa had suggested, and sitting with her back to his, she managed, although it was difficult and took a long time, to undo the knot at Jimmy's wrists.

Then by shaking and wriggling his hands as much as he could he got them free.

It took only a few minutes for him to release Mimosa.

Then as she shook her hands, feeling the blood coming back into her wrists and knowing how stiff her arms were, she said:

"I wonder why, if they were leaving us here, they took off our gags and the rest of our ropes?"

"I am jolly glad they did," Jimmy replied. "It was very uncomfortable and I was frightened."

"I am sure you were," Mimosa agreed, "and so was

I. But you have been very, very brave, and now we have to think how we can get out of here."

She looked around the horse-box and saw despite the fact that it was old, that it was very stoutly made.

She rose a little unsteadily to her feet and going to the door to try to push it open she soon realised that the bar she had heard being dropped into place was a strong one.

She was certain, however hard she and Jimmy might push against it, it would not break.

Then for the first time she had an idea of what her cousin intended to do with them.

For a moment it was so horrifying that she could not bear to work it out in her mind, and yet she knew almost as if she were seeing it clairvoyantly what he intended.

She and Jimmy had been brought in the horse-box to some isolated place, where it was very unlikely they would be found for at least a long time, if ever.

The noise she had heard on the roof and round the sides of the box had been the branches of trees being thrown over it in order to hide it.

This, then, was where they were to stay until they died of starvation, with no chance of being rescued.

The idea was so horrifying that as it came into her mind Mimosa wanted to scream for help and go on screaming.

Then she remembered the threat the man had made before they left, and she thought that although it had obviously been said to intimidate them and it was unlikely anyone would hear them scream, she dared not take the chance of being wrong for Jimmy's sake.

She knew that they had to escape, but she had no idea how they could do so.

How long would it take them to die?

She shut her eyes from the sheer horror of it. Then she heard Jimmy say, and she knew he was afraid:

"How are we to—get out of—here, Mimosa?"

As she dared not tell him she had no idea, she merely said:

"I think the first thing to do is to try to see if we can get out by that grating. Perhaps if it is at all loose, we might be able to pull it out."

She reckoned that somebody as small as Jimmy might be able to climb through the opening, but she was sure that the iron bars were firmly embedded in the wooden walls, and it would be impossible without the right tools even for a man with unusual strength to move it.

However, this was something she had no intention of saying aloud and she merely said:

"If you can climb up onto my shoulders, Jimmy, perhaps you could shake the bars and see how firm they are. At the same time, you could look outside to see where we are."

Jimmy started to do as she suggested.

He climbed onto his sister's shoulders, and with Mimosa holding his ankles to steady him, he reached up to hold on to the grating.

Even as she heard him touch it, she knew without being told how strong it was, and Jimmy exclaimed:

"The bars are quite firm and made of iron. All I can see outside are the branches of trees and some of them seem to be on top of us."

It was what Mimosa had already imagined, and when she did not speak, Jimmy gave the bars of the grating a shake and said:

"We cannot move these! We shall have to find another way out."

He jumped down as he spoke and Mimosa, looking

at him in his white flannel nightshirt, thought how small and vulnerable he was, and that unless by some miracle they were rescued, the horse-box would be turned into a tomb from which there was no escape.

She did not say this aloud but sat down again on the blanket and began to pray fervently that with the help of God the Marquis would find them.

Even as she prayed she thought that to search for them over the whole countryside would be like looking for a needle in a haystack.

The men had hidden the horse-box under branches so that anybody passing through the wood even close to where they were would be unlikely to notice them.

"At least we can scream then!" she told herself.

But this was little consolation, and she had the feeling that if she and Jimmy started to scream, it might make them even more afraid than they were at the moment.

'I must keep calm,' Mimosa thought, 'and not let Jimmy know how desperate our situation is.'

Jimmy sat down beside her.

"If we cannot get through the grating, Mimosa," he said, "how are we going to get out of here?"

"I do not know the answer to that question," Mimosa replied, trying to speak lightly.

Then because she was frightened, desperately frightened, she began to pray again, knowing as she did so that there was nothing else she could do.

*　　*　　*

By the time the Marquis had reached the stables he was having the greatest difficulty in dragging Hunter with him.

As they walked out into the Inner Courtyard, the dog pulled with all his strength on the lead in his anxiety to rush ahead out onto the drive outside.

It was only as they passed through the stone arch that the Marquis saw the wheel-marks on the gravel and realised there had been a vehicle waiting here into which the kidnappers must have put Mimosa and Jimmy.

Hunter confirmed what he was thinking by sniffing round the wheel-marks, then pulling once again in an effort to set off down the drive in the direction in which they must have gone.

The Marquis dragged him into the stables while he gave orders to the first groom he saw for two horses to be saddled immediately.

By the time they were led out of their stalls Charles had joined him.

"How can all this have happened without our hearing anything?" he asked.

"What we ought to have heard was Hunter," the Marquis replied, "but the walls are very thick and it was only during the night that I decided I would move Jimmy into my dressing-room."

"Well, it is too late to do that now," Charles said. "Where do you think they have been taken?"

"I have not the slightest idea," the Marquis answered. "We can only rely on Hunter."

He handed the dog's lead to one of the stable-boys and only when he and Charles were in the saddle did he tell the boy to let the dog go.

Hunter rushed, as the Marquis had expected he would, back to the Inner Courtyard and starting there, with his nose to the ground, began to move as quickly as his legs could carry him down the side drive.

Unlike the main drive, this led them through several grazing-fields and out of the Park onto a dusty lane with high hedgerows on either side.

The Marquis and Charles followed behind Hunter in silence.

The Marquis was scowling, and Charles knew he was extremely angry, not only for Mimosa's and Jimmy's sake, but also because he was blaming himself for underestimating his opponent.

It seemed extraordinary now that neither of them had thought for one moment that Norton Field would strike so quickly.

He had, in fact, been exceedingly clever. As soon as he had realised where Mimosa had gone for help, he had spirited Jimmy and his sister away before the Marquis was prepared for such immediate action.

The Marquis wanted to blame Charles for giving him the impression of a roué and a lecher rather than a hardheaded sharp-thinking criminal intent on stealing what he desired, whatever cost was involved in doing so.

Only a villain who was utterly despicable and perhaps more than slightly mad would have been ready to kill a young boy so that he could enjoy the benefits of his title.

The Marquis thought that until this moment he had in fact only half-believed Mimosa's story of her cousin's perfidy.

Field must have planned it all very carefully, and it struck the Marquis like a blow to be sure that it could not have happened without the help of some informer inside Heron.

This meant Norton Field must have bribed one of his own servants, and his fingers tightened on the reins as he thought with fury that he had always trusted his own staff implicitly and found it hard to believe they would let him down.

At the same time he had been abroad for a long period and many of the old servants had retired and had been replaced by those who were perhaps not so loyal or so proud of being employed in a big house in the way their predecessors had been.

It was all too easy, the Marquis thought, for somebody like Field to bribe a young footman, or even one of the scullions, not only with money, but by standing him drinks in the local Inn and flattering him by his attention.

Whatever the answer, Field had learnt very soon after Mimosa had left home where she had gone.

When she and Jimmy did not return, he must have realised that before the Marquis had time to organise their defence, he must strike quickly.

"Surprise is one of the best weapons of war," Wellington had said once.

The Marquis knew now that it was a weapon that Field had used very successfully.

All the time he was riding and thinking he was watching Hunter a little way ahead of them.

Sometimes the dog stopped, and when he did so the Marquis pulled in his horse and was exceedingly afraid that if Hunter lost the scent, they would have no idea where to go next.

He tried to think if he were in Norton Field's shoes where he would take Mimosa and Jimmy.

Neither of them were clothed except for their night attire, and unless Norton Field intended to kill them, bury them in some secluded spot, or drown them in a pond or stream, their appearance would preclude his taking them where they could be seen by any outsider.

Afraid that because he had abducted them in such a manner it was Field's intention to kill them, the Marquis's only consolation was Charles's argument that this was a most unlikely thing to happen.

This, of course, was because Norton Field could not run the risk in his position as heir presumptive of being suspected of murder.

The Marquis was growing more and more apprehensive as Hunter moved along the rough dirt-track that appeared to lead nowhere until ahead of him he saw there was a wood.

It was then that Charles, who had not spoken since they had left Heron, asked:

"Do you think the dog knows what he is doing?"

"We have no other clue," the Marquis said sharply.

Then as he looked ahead he said:

"I have just realised this is my boundary."

Charles looked at him in surprise.

"Your boundary?" he asked. "Then who does the wood belong to?"

"The Earl of Petersfield!"

The two men looked at each other, and the Marquis said:

"It makes some sort of sense. If he is hiding Mimosa and Jimmy on their own ground, he will be familiar with it, and the estate is certainly not as well looked after as mine."

Now they were drawing nearer to the wood and the Marquis added:

"Now I think of it, I remember one of my keepers complaining to me of the quantity of vermin in the Earl's woods. They are a menace to our own birds because since he has been ill there has been no shooting and the game-keepers have been dismissed."

"What you are saying," Charles said, watching Hunter running ahead of them, "is that there must be dozens of isolated places on the Earl of Petersfield's estate where Field could hide two young people, and it would be very hard to find them."

"Very hard indeed!" the Marquis said in a serious voice.

Now the dirt-track which Hunter had been following over the fields entered the wood, and ahead of them the Marquis saw there was a rough ride.

The ground was bumpy and covered with fallen twigs and branches of trees, and he could see that the wood was in a disgraceful state.

Dead trees fallen into the undergrowth and left to rot there, and those which were growing were far too close together for the trees to develop as they should.

There was also, as his game-keeper had told him, an inordinate number of jays and magpies, which fluttered away as they appeared and seemed almost to resent their intrusion.

"The place is certainly neglected!" Charles said unnecessarily.

The Marquis did not reply. He thought perhaps it would be a mistake to talk in case Field or his men were lurking in the wood, and would be alerted to their presence.

At the same time he was certain that with several hours start, Field, or whoever had kidnapped Mimosa and Jimmy, would surely no longer be in the vicinity of their crime if they had killed the two young people.

Nor would they be hanging about if they had imprisoned them in some cave or perhaps a wood-cutter's hut.

He had thought when he was a boy that the many wood-cutters' huts which were to be found in the woods around Heron made excellent hiding-places, and on several occasions he had hidden in one of them to avoid his Tutors.

Then he had heard, with satisfaction, them calling to him while they had no idea he was actually quite near them.

He glanced at the trees on either side as they still followed Hunter, but as they were all close together with no clearing, there was no sign of the hut he was seeking.

It would be made of trunks of trees split down the middle, and fixed so close to each other that the hut when completed was rain-proof and comparatively warm in the winter months.

Then ahead of them unexpectedly Hunter stopped.

Now he seemed lost, moving from first one side of the ride, then to the other, and the Marquis's heart sank.

He was well aware that this wood was very large and spread over a great number of acres.

It could take them days to search it thoroughly, and although if he really believed this was where Mimosa and Jimmy were hidden, he would go back to Heron and bring every available man to assist him in his search, he was not optimistic of being quickly successful.

Hunter was casting round in circles and the Marquis dismounted, handing as he did so his horse's bridle to Charles

"If Hunter has lost the scent, what are we going to do?" Charles asked, but the Marquis did not reply.

He only moved to where Hunter, breathless from the speed at which he had run, was sniffing the ground and still moving from side to side of the ride.

The Marquis looked down on the ground, and now he could see the faint marks of the wheels on the grass, and they appeared to have come to a stop.

What puzzled him, as it obviously was puzzling Hunter, was that there appeared to be no turning off from the ride itself.

On one side there were trees growing very close together, while on the other a mass of undergrowth and fallen branches created a barrier which seemed for the moment impassable.

Then the Marquis noticed something which was significant.

Some of the branches which lay at the side of the ride had only recently been cut from a tree.

He pulled them to one side and immediately Hunter began to scratch his way through the small aperture he had made.

The Marquis moved more of the boughs, and as the dog seemed to understand he was helping him, he tried to nose his way under a number of other branches.

The Marquis turned his head.

"Come and help me, Charles! You can leave the horses. I do not think they will stray far."

Charles dismounted and knotted the reins of each horse at the neck.

They immediately put down their heads and began to crop the grass and Charles felt there would be no difficulty about catching them again.

He then joined the Marquis, helping him to move the branches of the trees while Hunter pushed his way ahead of them.

Then suddenly they saw it.

It was so covered in branches that they were right

against it before they realised it was there: a strange old-fashioned square horse-box wedged between two trees.

The Marquis looked at Charles without speaking, then feeling as if he turned over the last card in the pack, he shouted:

"Is anyone there?"

For a moment there was only silence. Then there were two voices crying at once:

"Help! Help us! Please . . . let us . . . out!"

The voices were rather faint, as if those inside were afraid to speak.

Then as the Marquis replied: "It is all right—we are here to save you!" he heard Jimmy's shrill little voice crying out in excitement.

He also thought, although he was not certain, that as he and Charles raised the bar on the door, he heard Mimosa saying:

"Thank You, God, thank You!"

*　　*　　*

It took the Marquis and Charles only a few seconds to lift the bar and open the doors of the horse-box.

But before they could get them fully open, Hunter sprang in, yelping with excitement and jumping up at Mimosa, and as she put her arms round him the tears were running down her cheeks.

It was Jimmy who moved first and jumped into Charles's arms, as he was nearest to him.

"You have come! You have come!" he cried. "We were so afraid no one would ever find us."

"We have indeed found you!" Charles replied. "But you have to thank Hunter, for he was the only one clever enough to know where you had gone."

"It has been very frightening!" Jimmy said, putting his arms round Charles's neck.

"I am sure it has," Charles answered, "and we will get you back to Heron as quickly as possible. I am sure you are hungry!"

"Very hungry!" Jimmy agreed. "I could eat a dozen sausages!"

It took Mimosa a little while to ward off Hunter's attentions before she could move towards the Marquis.

He waited for her, and only as she met his eyes did she seem to realise how little she was wearing and that her thin nightgown was very revealing.

The tears were still on her cheeks, but she gave him a brave little smile before she bent down and picked up the blanket in which she had been carried off and put it over her shoulders.

As she did so the Marquis held out his arms and lifted her out of the horse-box.

He realised that her feet were bare and said:

"As it is not possible for you to walk, I will carry you."

Mimosa was looking up at him, her eyelashes wet from her tears, her eyes very expressive as she said:

"You came! I prayed to God that by some . . . miracle you would . . . find us . . . but I could not . . . think how you would be able to . . . do so."

"You forgot Hunter," the Marquis said. "He must take all the credit. If he had not led us here, we would not have had the slightest idea what that fiend had done with you."

"How could it have happened at . . . Heron?"

"That is what I have been asking myself," the Marquis

said angrily, "and it is something that will never happen again. That I promise you!"

"I think," Mimosa said in a very small voice, "that Cousin Norton intended us to . . . starve to death . . . so that it would be impossible for anyone to lay the blame on him . . . for having murdered us."

"I am sure that is what he intended," the Marquis agreed. "But we have managed to stop such a terrible thing from happening, so do not think about it until you are safely back at Heron and have had something to eat."

"I . . . I might have . . . known you would . . . save us," Mimosa said in a shaky little voice.

As the Marquis did not answer, she thought perhaps he had not heard her.

Charles had already caught the horses and Jimmy was sitting in the front of his saddle.

The Marquis lifted Mimosa onto his horse and mounted behind her, putting his left arm round her to hold her close against him.

It was then for the first time, because the relief of getting away was so intense, she felt a little faint, and shutting her eyes, she put her head against the Marquis's shoulder.

As if he knew what she was feeling, he said very quietly:

"It is all right—it is all over now, and it is going to be a long time before he realises you have escaped."

"When they go back later," Mimosa said in a frightened little voice, "they will . . . know it was you . . . who found us."

It ran through the Marquis's mind that if there was, as he suspected, somebody at Heron who was in league with Norton Field, he would be informed of his prisoners' escape without having to return to look in the horse-box.

The idea made him very angry, but there was nothing he could do at the moment, and he could therefore only ride carefully, so as not to shake Mimosa any more than was unavoidable, back to Heron.

As they went Jimmy was chatting away to Charles, telling him exactly what had happened since he had been awakened by feeling a hand over his mouth.

He described how frightening it had been when he and Mimosa had discovered there was no way they could get out of the horse-box.

Mimosa did not feel like talking.

She only sat limply in the Marquis's arms, and as they rode on he had the feeling that she was so deeply grateful that she and her brother were not to die that she was thanking God in her heart.

He glanced down at her and thought she looked very young and vulnerable and as he did so, she opened her eyes and looked up at him and said:

"H-how can I . . . ever thank you for . . . s-saving Jimmy?"

The way she spoke was so intense that the Marquis deliberately replied lightly:

"I told you—you must thank Hunter!"

There was a little pause, then Mimosa said:

"How can we . . . possibly live . . . knowing this may h-happen again and again until Cousin Norton is . . . successful?"

It was a question the Marquis had been asking himself, and he knew that for the moment he had no answer.

chapter five

"IT is obvious that we must have an early night after such an over-dramatic day," the Marquis said dryly.

As he spoke he noticed that Jimmy's eyelids were dropping and also that Mimosa looked very tired.

There was so much to talk about, so much to relate to each other, that there had been no chance of resting after they returned to Heron.

By the time Jimmy and Mimosa had eaten a large breakfast, bathed, and dressed, it was almost time for luncheon, and after that they went on talking and, of course, planning.

"What are we going to do now?" Charles asked pertinently. "So far the enemy has won on points, even if we have managed to prevent him from gaining a victory."

He thought as he spoke how easy it would have been for Norton Field to have destroyed Jimmy and Mimosa as he had planned to do, had not it been for Hunter, who had tracked down his mistress.

They had reasoned out amongst themselves exactly how Field had planned what had been a clever operation.

"Nobody goes into that wood of Grandpapa's," Mimosa said, "for the simple reason that the trees have never done well, and after Grandpapa gave up shooting, we lost all our gamekeepers."

"I know that to my cost," the Marquis said ruefully. "My keepers complain bitterly about the enormous amount of vermin it harbours."

"The wood is so very big," Mimosa sighed, "and there is a gravel pit on one side of it which was used, I believe, in Roman times. When it rains it fills with water and is dangerous to animals, so the farmers keep well away."

It was obvious as she spoke that there was no attraction for anyone to visit the wood, and it was astute of Norton Field to have thought of leaving them there and concealing their presence so that if by chance there was a casual passer-by, he would not notice it.

"What I do not understand," Charles remarked, "is why the men who kidnapped them took off their gags and ropes for those round their wrists."

"I too thought that was strange," Mimosa agreed.

"He obviously guessed," the Marquis replied, "that they would be able to release their wrists. Then when their corpses were found there would be nothing to indicate there had been any criminal intent to murder them."

Charles looked at him in astonishment.

"How can you say that?" he asked. "They were locked in!"

"The bar on the door could have been lifted at any time after they were dead. Their night-clothes would doubtless have crumbled away."

The Marquis pondered as if he were working it out before he went on:

"If they were found in a year or so, when Norton Field was applying to be acknowledged as the Fifth Earl owing to Jimmy's disappearance, it would be difficult to find any motive for Mimosa and Jimmy to be hidden in the wood unless they went there themselves and in some extraordinary manner were unable to get away."

"I can see what you are saying," Charles said, "and it has some sort of reasoning about it."

"It has merely convinced me, if I were not convinced already, that Field has an astute brain which is twisted, diabolical, and undoubtedly mad," the Marquis said harshly. "At the same time, I agree with you—he is clever."

"Then what . . . can we . . . do?" Mimosa asked fearfully.

"That is what I am going to think out very carefully," the Marquis replied. "We are all tired, and we shall be able to approach the problem more objectively tomorrow after a good night's sleep."

They went upstairs together, because the Marquis had said he wanted to supervise all the arrangements, particularly as to where Jimmy would be sleeping.

Charles's room came first, and he went into it. They then came to Mimosa's.

As she opened the door she hesitated and said:

"I think I would be happier if tonight Hunter slept with Jimmy. If somebody crept in and prevented him from calling out as they did last night, Hunter would wake you."

"That is a good idea," the Marquis agreed, "but will he stay with Jimmy?"

Mimosa smiled.

"If I tell him to."

She bent down to pat Hunter, who was standing beside her, and said:

"Go with Jimmy, Hunter. On guard! There is a good dog!"

For a moment Hunter hesitated, looking at her, longing to be with the mistress he adored.

Then Jimmy said:

"Come on, Hunter! Come and sleep on my bed as you sometimes do at home."

"On guard, Hunter!" Mimosa said again.

The dog, with what seemed like a reproachful look at her, moved slowly towards Jimmy, who began to run ahead down the corridor.

Hunter ran after him, and Mimosa smiled at the Marquis.

"Good night," she said, "and thank you for bringing us home safely."

As the Marquis walked away he heard the key turn in the lock.

Henson had everything arranged for Jimmy to sleep in the dressing-room which opened directly into the Marquis's bedroom, and he was there waiting for them.

"Help His Lordship into bed," the Marquis said. "He is half-asleep already. Then, Henson, there will be no need for you to come back, as I intend to read the newspaper before I go to bed."

"When I've 'ad me supper, M'Lord, I'll be back an' see if there's anythin' I can do for you," Henson said firmly.

The Marquis did not argue, but picked up a newspaper and settled himself in an armchair.

It took Henson only a few minutes to help Jimmy undress, then having drawn the curtains, he came into the Marquis's room, leaving the door ajar.

"I am sure there will be no trouble tonight," the Marquis said, "but you have put my pistol by my bed?"

"Yes, M'Lord, an' o' course it's loaded!"

"Good!"

When he was alone, instead of reading *The Times*, which he held in his hand, the Marquis rose to stand at the window looking out onto the garden.

The sun was sinking, but there was still a vivid glow behind the trees, and it was that quiet moment of dusk when the first evening star was coming out faintly in the translucence of the sky.

There was no sound except for the high squeak of a bat and the last of the rooks going to roost in the oak trees in the Park.

It seemed impossible, with everything so peaceful and beautiful, that there could be a villain like Norton Field plotting and planning to murder a young boy simply because he wanted his title.

The Marquis felt his whole body tense with his determination to outwit him, and yet he had to face the fact that so far it was only by a miraculous stroke of luck and not by any brilliance on his part that Norton Field had been unsuccessful.

"What the devil do we do next?" he asked.

Then, as if he forced himself not to go on worrying, he sat down again in the armchair and putting his feet up on a stool deliberately opened a newspaper at the Editorial.

* * *

Mimosa was also looking at the beauty of the last golden rays of the sun.

She had pulled back the curtains from one of the high windows in her bedroom and pushed up the lower part of the window as far as it would go.

Then she looked out, thinking, as the Marquis had, how beautiful everything was and how it seemed impossible there should be evil so near them and the menacing fingers of death when everything appeared to be so quiet and peaceful.

'This is the third time that Jimmy has been saved,' she thought to herself. 'What will Cousin Norton try next?'

She felt herself shiver at the thought of him, then turned from the window and started to undress.

There was a small wardrobe room leading out of her bedroom which must have been designed originally as a Powder Closet.

She took off her evening-gown and hung it up, thinking as she did so how dull and ordinary she must have looked in it beside the treasures of Heron and the distinguished appearance of the Marquis and Charles in their evening-clothes.

"Perhaps one day," she told herself, "when nothing frightening is happening, I shall be able to buy a gown in which I would not look so countrified and so dull."

The only reason she wanted to look different was to make the Marquis admire her as he admired the beautiful women with whom he associated in London.

She had heard about them from Henson, who had, of

course, been very voluble on the subject.

"His Lordship must find it very dull here in the country when he does not have a party," Mimosa had said.

"He had a large party just before you arrived, M'Lady," Henson answered.

"Were the ladies very elegantly dressed and very beautiful?" Mimosa asked because she could not suppress her curiosity.

"They glittered all over with diamonds like chandeliers," Henson answered with a grin, "and wore gowns that must have cost a mint o' money!"

"And were they witty and amusing?"

"That's the way they all starts," Henson replied, "but they soon gets 'Is Lordship yawning, then—hey, presto!—they disappear out of his life and in comes another!"

Mimosa had the idea she should not allow Henson to talk to her like this, but she could not help finding it fascinating.

She wanted to know more about the Marquis's likes and dislikes, simply because she had never thought it possible there could be a man like him.

He was so clever and interesting and at the same time so kind and understanding.

"No one else would have listened to me when I came here with such a fantastic story," she told herself, "and no one else would have cared for Jimmy and me as he is doing now."

She wondered what he actually thought about them both except as a challenge and, as Charles had said, a campaign.

Then as she shut the wardrobe door she found herself thinking:

'Perhaps if I had just one really pretty gown he would admire me.'

She did not ask herself why that was what she wanted, but when she walked back into her bedroom wearing only her nightgown she was thinking of the Marquis.

She looked in the mirror, seeing not her own, but his handsome face.

She knew she should sit down and brush her hair with a hundred strokes as her mother had taught her to do.

Instead, she walked again to the window to have one last look at the gold of the sky and the shadows growing longer under the trees before she got into bed.

But as she did so the curtains that were drawn over the other window parted and a man came into the room.

Mimosa made an effort to scream, but no sound would come to her lips as she saw that it was Norton Field, who was confronting her.

"Do not make a sound, Mimosa," he said sharply, "or I shall have to gag you again!"

"What . . . are you . . . doing? W-why are you . . . h-here?" Mimosa asked incoherently.

"I want to talk to you, and I think it is unlikely that we shall be disturbed."

There was a mocking note in his voice that made her feel he was more menacing, more evil even than she remembered.

Then as she stood staring at him, her eyes wide and frightened, her hands instinctively going to her breasts, she realised as he looked at her that her nightgown was very thin and transparent and, in the light from the window, very revealing.

She looked quickly for her dressing gown, which a maid would have left for her over a chair, but with a smile that had something sinister about it Norton Field said:

"Get into bed, Mimosa! I can talk to you there as well as anywhere else."

Because she was so frightened she moved away from him in her bare feet and climbed into the huge four-poster, pulling the sheets closely around her.

He followed her across the room, taking off his coat on the way and throwing it down on a chair.

When he reached her and sat on the side of the mattress, she felt herself shrink from him, feeling the evil vibrating towards her almost as if she could see it.

Norton Field did not speak, and after a moment Mimosa asked in a frightened whisper:

"H-how did you ... know we were ... b-back here?"

"I am not answering questions, Mimosa, but I will tell you what I intend to do."

She supposed he was going to tell her how he now intended to kill Jimmy, and she clasped her fingers so tightly together that they went white.

"As you have prevented me from destroying Jimmy as I had planned," Norton Field said, "I now have another idea which I think might even commend itself to you!"

She knew he was mocking her once again, and she managed to ask angrily:

"How can you ... talk of ... destroying Jimmy? It is evil ... and ... wicked! And if you do ... so you will be caught ... and hanged ... which is what ... you deserve!"

Norton Field laughed, and it was not a pretty sound.

"Quite a little spitfire! And actually I have to agree with you. Murder in the circumstances of your having brought the Most Noble Marquis into the picture might be rather dangerous. That is why I have something different to suggest, which will at least allow your precious brother to live a little longer than I first intended."

"What do you . . . mean? What . . . are you talking . . . about?" Mimosa asked.

"Today, when I left you to die, as you should have done in the wood," Norton Field replied, "I thought it was rather a pity that anybody so attractive and with such a lovely body should just decompose."

"So it was . . . you who . . . touched me!"

Now as she remembered how she had felt a man's hand move first down one side of her body, then the other, the colour came into her cheeks with embarrassment, because she had been wearing so little at the time.

"Yes, it was I," Norton Field said, "and it was then it struck me that I might have arranged things rather differently, which is what I am going to do now."

"And . . . what is . . . that?"

Even as she asked the question, Mimosa shrank in fear from the answer.

It would be something she did not wish to hear, and she knew perceptively it would be horrible, degrading, and terrifying.

"What I intend to do," Norton Field said, "is to marry you!"

Whatever Mimosa had expected, it was not this, and instinctively she sat more upright against her pillows and for a moment she could only stare at him until she asked:

"What are you . . . saying? Is this . . . some sort of a joke?"

"It is no joke," Norton Field replied. "Because you interfered with my arrangements which I had thought to be foolproof, we will now tackle things in a slightly different way. I will marry you, Mimosa, and that will automatically make me, with you, Jimmy's Guardian until he comes of age!

"We will live comfortably in the style to which the Earls of Petersfield are accustomed. I will administer the estate and see that it becomes more productive than it is at the moment, and I will in fact have nearly all the privileges of being the Fifth Earl until that is what I actually become."

His eyes narrowed for a moment, and looking at him in horror, Mimosa knew he was thinking that long before Jimmy came of age, it would be quite easy for him by some means or other to arrange his death.

There was silence, and knowing that Norton Field was waiting for her to speak, with what was a super-human effort she defied him.

"You must be crazy if you think for one moment I would . . . marry you!" she said. "I loathe and detest you! You are a criminal, a . . . murderer, and sooner or later you will be . . . punished for your . . . crimes."

"I am not giving up, and you will not prevent me from doing what I want," he replied. "What is more, our relatives will think it a very sensible idea for you to have a husband like me, your cousin, to help you look after Jimmy, and have the interests of the family at heart."

"The only interest you have is yourself," Mimosa snapped, "and I know that you intend to take Jimmy's place! Do you really think that as your . . . wife I would connive at anything so . . . horrible or so . . . wicked as to see my own brother . . . murdered?"

"You are behaving as I expected," Norton Field replied. "As I have already said, you have no choice. You will either agree to do what I want without making a fuss, or I will force you to obey me."

"You may drag me to the altar, but you cannot make me say that I will be your wife," Mimosa answered. "It would be a farce that would soil the sacredness of the word for you to ask for the blessing of God on your marriage!"

Norton Field did not answer but was looking at her with a sinister smile on his lips which made her more afraid than if he had raged at her.

"And however clever you may be," Mimosa said, "you cannot make me say I will be your wife."

"You will say it when the time comes," Norton Field replied, "and what is more, I find it amusing that you are spitting at me like a wildcat. But I will tame you, make no mistake about that!"

"In the meantime, ask yourself why I have come to your room tonight."

The way he spoke swept for a moment anything she was about to say from her lips.

Then as she stared at him, her eyes dark with fear, he moved towards her and said:

"After tonight, Mimosa, you will have no choice as to whether you will marry me, because I shall already have made you mine!"

With a swift movement for which she was completely unprepared, he pulled the sheets away from her and flung himself on top of her.

For a moment she could hardly believe it was happening.

Then as she felt the weight of his body and his hands tearing at her nightgown, she screamed.

It was the sound of a terrified animal caught in a trap.

* * *

The Marquis finished reading the Editorial in *The Times* and the report of a debate in the House of Lords at which he himself ought to have been present.

Then as his hand went towards *The Morning Post* he decided he might as well undress and get into bed.

By now the light was fading outside, but he thought he would not light the candles in case he attracted the flies.

Instead, he took off his evening-coat and put it on a chair and was just removing his cravat when suddenly the door burst open and Henson rushed into the room.

His breath was coming fitfully from between his lips as he exclaimed:

"M'Lord! M'Lord!"

"What is it?" the Marquis asked, turning from the mirror over his chest of drawers in front of which he had been undressing.

"I've discovered who's been informing Mr. Field of the young Lordship's movements!"

The Marquis was still.

"Someone in the house?" he asked sharply.

"The pantry boy, M'Lord! It was 'im who let the—men in last night by the door into the Inner Courtyard. I hears 'im jingling the—sovereigns in his pocket—and I forced it—out of 'im! An' he says he's received—another five of them—tonight for—letting Mr. Field into the—house!"

"He is in the house now? At this moment?" the Marquis asked.

"Yes, M'Lord!"

It was still hard for Henson to speak, and he could only gasp:

"Mr. Field's with—Her Ladyship! He—went to her—room while you was at—dinner!"

For a moment the Marquis stared at Henson as if he felt he could not have heard him aright.

Then he moved swiftly across the bedroom, picked up the pistol beside his bed, and ran out into the passage.

As he did so he remembered that he had heard Mimosa lock her door and realised that Field must have been already concealed inside her room when she did so.

He therefore opened the door of the *boudoir*, which was next to his own room, and moving carefully across it in the darkness because the curtains were drawn, he had almost reached the communicating door when he heard Mimosa screaming.

He opened the door and as he did so Mimosa screamed again, not loudly but with the smothered sound of abject terror.

Her voice came from the bed, and as the Marquis saw what was happening, and Field's body lying on top of hers, he threw his pistol down on a chair.

He then sprang with the agility of an athlete at the man he had been wanting to catch.

The Marquis was very strong, and Field was at a disadvantage in that he was facing down on the bed.

Nevertheless, he struggled violently until the Marquis, picking him up in his arms with a superhuman strength inspired by his fury at what he had seen, carried him bodily across the room and flung him out of the open window.

Norton Field yelled as he did so, and yelled again as he fell.

Then, as he hit the ground, the Marquis did not wait to see what had happened to him, but turned back towards the bed.

Mimosa was sitting up, pulling her torn nightgown

over her bare breasts, trembling violently with the shock of what had happened.

The Marquis moved towards her, and as he did so he realised that Henson had followed him in through the communicating door.

"See to that swine outside, Henson!" the Marquis said sharply. "And whether he is dead or alive, get him off my property!"

He knew he did not have to explain to Henson why this was important.

Without saying a word, the valet ran across the room in front of the Marquis, unlocked the bedroom door leading to the passage, and went out, closing it behind him.

The Marquis reached Mimosa and as he looked down at her in what was now a very dim light he said:

"It is all right! He will never trouble you again. You must try to forget this has happened."

It was not what he said, but the kindness in his voice that penetrated through the horror that had left Mimosa quivering with fear.

Then as the Marquis sat down on the bed she burst into tears.

His arms went around her and he held her close against him, saying quietly:

"It is all right, Mimosa! It is all over! Both you and Jimmy are safe now."

He realised as he spoke that she was past hearing or understanding anything he said.

She was crying tempestuously, like a child who had lost control, and was aware only of her own misery.

The Marquis could feel her tears seeping through his fine linen shirt, but there was nothing he could do but hold her so that she felt safe because he was there.

"It is all right!" he said again. "You have been very, very brave, but now you must forget all this ever happened."

Slowly, and it took a long time, her weeping began to subside, and her tears were no longer so tempestuous.

"It is all over!" the Marquis reiterated. "Now I shall be able to see you smiling and happy without that worried look in your eyes that has been there ever since we first met."

There was a little pause, then Mimosa asked:

"Is—is he . . . dead?"

"I hope so!" the Marquis replied savagely. "But it will be more convenient for everybody and will save a lot of unpleasant questions if he can be found somewhere else than on my estate. We shall know more when Henson comes back."

"H-he . . . terrified me!" Mimosa said in a very small voice. "He is . . . horrible . . . disgusting!"

"I know," the Marquis agreed, "but I arrived in time, and all you have to do now is to forget he ever touched you."

Mimosa shivered. It shook her whole body and the Marquis went on:

"Just understand that he is mad, deranged—an animal who did not know what he was doing."

"H-H . . . said I . . . had to . . . m-marry him."

The Marquis stiffened in astonishment.

"Marry him? But why?"

"So that . . . he could be Jimmy's . . . legal Guardian until such time as he . . . decided to k-kill him!"

The Marquis thought this was something he had not anticipated.

He blamed himself for not having been quick enough to foresee such a clever idea, for if Field had had complete power over Jimmy, he could plan with very little difficulty how to become, as he intended, the Fifth Earl of Petersfield.

Aloud to soothe Mimosa he said:

"Whatever plans he had can be forgotten, and you know, Mimosa, he will never trouble you again. Of that I am certain!"

Mimosa could only cling to him. Then she said:

"He . . . said that . . . after tonight . . . I would be . . . obliged to m-marry him . . . as I would have . . . no choice. Then he flung himself on me . . . but . . . but I did not . . . understand what he m-meant."

The Marquis was still for a moment as he realised that in her innocence Mimosa honestly had no idea what Field had intended.

She was only disgusted and horrified by the fact that he had been tearing at her nightgown and touching her naked body.

Because he did not want her to go on puzzling over something which no one had explained to her, he said soothingly:

"Field has a reputation for being a Roué, and I can only imagine that tonight, after telling you he intended to marry you, he found you so attractive that he did not wish to wait to kiss you."

"He did not . . . k-kiss me!" Mimosa replied. "He just tore my nightgown . . . and . . . lay on . . . t-top of me!"

"You must not think about it anymore," the Marquis said sharply. "He must have had too much to drink, and anyway, he is a man who has no idea of how to behave like a gentleman, apart from the fact that he was intent on committing a murder!"

He knew that Mimosa was still puzzled, and he said:

"You have been so brave up to now, and I do not

know any woman who would have behaved so splendidly as you have done, especially after having been gagged, bound, and shut up in that horse-box."

"I was . . . frightened!" Mimosa said. "But not as . . . frightened as I was with . . . Cousin Norton just now."

The Marquis could understand what she was feeling, and he knew he had to reassure her.

"If you go to pieces now, what shall I do about Jimmy?" he asked. "You have to be brave not only for your own sake, but also for his. Never mind if it seems rather improper that we should celebrate the fact that your cousin is finally disposed of, and that we can be assured that we will not have to worry about him in the future."

He paused before he said in a lighter and slightly teasing tone:

"I cannot believe you have any more cousins who are equally abominable?"

"No, of course not!" Mimosa said. "And it has just occurred to me that it would be a mistake to . . . upset Jimmy. He must not know what . . . happened here . . . tonight."

"I was thinking that it would be best to prevent anyone from knowing," the Marquis said. "I am going to look out of the window, Mimosa, and see if I can see anything."

The Marquis took his arms from her, and as she moved back against her pillows, she did so reluctantly.

Then, as he rose from the bed he drew the sheets Field had pulled away back over her and knew, although it was dark, that she pulled them up to her chin.

He walked to the window but could see no sign of Norton Field on the ground below, nor of Henson, for that matter.

He had fancied, however, that he heard, while Mimosa was crying in his arms, the sound of wheels moving away.

As he thought of it, there was a knock at the door, and before he could answer, Henson came into the bedroom.

"It's all right, M'Lord."

"What have you done?" the Marquis asked.

Henson joined him at the window.

"When I gets to 'im he was breathing, but unconscious, M'Lord. But I thinks he'd broken his back and one of his arms, and there were a nasty gash on his forehead where he'd hit the ground, which was pouring blood all down 'is face."

The Marquis did not speak, but was listening as Henson went on:

"I lifts 'im into his carriage and there was only one 'orse and an elderly man to drive 'im who asks me what's 'appened."

"'Your master's 'ad an accident,' I replied. 'Get 'im back to where you're staying, an' send for a doctor, and 'urry up about it!'"

Henson's voice changed as he added:

"He drove off quick, M'Lord, but I wouldn't mind bettin' that Mr. Field won't be alive when he reaches his destination."

"Good!" the Marquis said. "Who knows what has happened except ourselves?"

"No one, M'Lord," Henson replied. "There is nobody as sleeps in the front of the house, as Your Lordship well knows. All the staff windows open in the other direction."

The Marquis nodded, and Henson went on:

"The groom, or whoever the man is who's drivin' Mr. Field, may try to accuse us, but we can just deny it, and it'll be his word against ours."

"Thank you, Henson. You have been excellent, as always!" the Marquis said.

Henson grinned and went through the communicating door of the *boudoir*.

The Marquis lit a candle by the bedside, then walked across the room to pull the curtains.

When he turned again, all he could see of Mimosa was her eyes, very large, looking at him from above the sheet with which he had covered her.

"I—I heard what Henson told you," she said as he sat down again beside her, "so there is ... nothing to ... worry about."

"There is nothing to upset you any longer," the Marquis confirmed.

"I can hardly believe it!" Mimosa whispered.

"You will believe it in the morning when you find the world a much cleaner place now your cousin is no longer in it."

"And Jimmy is safe."

"Yes, of course, Jimmy is safe, and so are you!"

He smiled and added:

"When I have gone, blow out the candle and try to get some sleep. Just remember, if anything should frighten you, Jimmy and I are only two doors away from you."

She smiled at him, and he knew now it did not demand the effort it had before.

"You ... s-saved me!" she whispered.

"Once and for all!" the Marquis added. "And it is something I will not have to do again. Good night, Mimosa. Just remember that everything is now 'plain sailing' and you and Jimmy are free to be happy."

"I will...try to remember...that," Mimosa answered, and she smiled at him again as he reached the door.

Then, as she heard him going along the passage to his own bedroom, she felt the tears coming into her eyes again, but this time they were tears of happiness and relief.

She was safe, and the Marquis was even more wonderful than she had already thought him to be.

"I love him," she murmured, and it seemed only right and natural that she should do so.

chapter six

WHEN Mimosa and Jimmy came down to breakfast, they found only Charles was there.

"Are you feeling better?" he asked.

"Much better, thank you," Mimosa answered.

"Has anything else happened?" Jimmy asked excitedly, and Charles shook his head.

When they had chosen something to eat from the long array of silver entree dishes on the sideboard, they sat down at the table and as they did so, the Marquis came into the room.

He glanced around as if to make sure no servants were present, then he said:

"I have just learned that after an accident Norton Field

died half-an-hour ago at the Posting Inn on the main road where he was staying."

For a moment there was silence. Then Jimmy exclaimed:

"That means he cannot try to kill me anymore!"

"That is true," the Marquis replied. "At the same time, I have ordered a carriage to come round immediately to take you and your sister home."

Mimosa stared at him wide-eyed and he explained:

"It is important that when the doctor who has been in attendance on your cousin notifies you that he is dead, he should not in any way connect him or you with Heron."

"No! Of course . . . I understand," Mimosa said in a low voice.

The Marquis then looked at Charles.

"You and I, Charles," he said, "are also leaving for London."

"I think that is sensible," Charles agreed.

"We must therefore all look exceedingly surprised when we are told of Norton Field's death from some accident which nobody can explain. You, Jimmy, will attend the funeral, which will, of course, be very quiet, but there is no need for your sister to go."

Mimosa gave a little sigh of relief.

Then, when the Marquis would have gone on speaking, the door from the Pantry opened and a servant came in, bringing a fresh pot of coffee which he set beside his Master.

To change the subject, Charles remarked:

"I have just seen in *The Times* that Sir Alexander Barclay has arrived at 60 Park Street. That should mean an end to the Army of Occupation."

"A good thing too!" the Marquis replied in the same

conversational tone. "Our soldiers had too little to do and the French hated us."

As he finished speaking, the servant left the room and Mimosa rose from the table.

"If we are to leave at once," she said, "I had better go upstairs and get ready."

"I have already given orders for your things to be packed," the Marquis said, "and yours and mine, Charles, will follow us with Henson."

It was a quarter-of-an-hour later when Mimosa came downstairs with a shawl over her muslin gown and a plain chip-straw bonnet on her fair hair.

She had found, as the Marquis had said, that everything was already packed for her and there was really nothing to do once she had put on her bonnet but say good-bye to the most beautiful bedroom in which she had ever slept, and to Heron itself.

It had been a strange visit, she thought, with moments of sheer terror, and others in which it had seemed as if she had been carried away into a Fairyland of beauty and happiness.

The latter, she knew, was entirely due to the Marquis, and she thought as she stood at the window out of which he had thrown Norton Field to his death that she had loved him almost from the first moment she had seen him.

She had only been a child then, and yet she had been unable to forget his handsome face and the impact of his personality.

"I love him!" she told the lake gleaming in the sunshine.

"I love him!" she said to the oak trees under which the roe deer were already sheltering from the heat.

And yet she knew despairingly that never again was she likely to be invited to Heron.

Never again would she feel the wonder of the Marquis's arms around her and know that he had saved not only Jimmy from the terror and menace of Norton Field, but also herself.

"Could any man be more wonderful?" she asked.

She felt, now that she must say good-bye to him, that the Fairy-Story in which she had been living since coming to Heron had come to an abrupt and tragic end.

Finally, as Jimmy called her, she turned away from the window to look at the exquisitely carved and gilded bed in which she had slept.

For a moment she did not remember the horror of being kidnapped or of Norton Field lying on top of her, tearing at her nightgown.

Instead, she thought of the comfort and security of the Marquis's arms when she had cried uncontrollably on his shoulder.

"Mimosa! The horses are waiting!" Jimmy called again from the top of the stairs.

Mimosa took one last look around the room in which so many dramatic things had happened, but which she felt still held the dignity it had commanded for centuries, before she replied:

"I am coming, Jimmy!"

With Hunter beside her she joined him at the top of the stairs, and they walked down them hand-in-hand to where the Marquis and Charles were waiting for them in the Hall below.

"His Lordship has already sent our horses home with two grooms," Jimmy said.

"That is right," the Marquis agreed as they reached him. "I thought it proper for you to go home in style, and I am sure you will find my carriage very comfortable."

"I would much rather have ridden one of your horses," Jimmy replied. "Will I ever have a chance of riding one again?"

Mimosa put her hand on her brother's shoulder.

"You must not ask anything like that," she admonished him gently, "after His Lordship has been so kind to us."

"I expect you will have your own later," the Marquis said after what Mimosa thought was an embarrassing pause, "and as we are neighbours, we shall be bound to see each other in the future. Take care of your sister, Jimmy."

He saw as he finished speaking that Jimmy was looking disappointed, and he turned quickly to Mimosa to say:

"Good-bye, Mimosa! I am glad everything has turned out so satisfactorily."

"If it has, it is entirely due to you, My Lord," Mimosa replied, "and you know ... how very, very grateful ... we are."

She found it difficult to speak calmly because tears were about to spill from her eyes.

As if the Marquis were aware of it, he turned towards the open door where the footmen were waiting on top of the steps.

Slowly Mimosa moved down them, and Charles, who was walking beside her, said, as they reached the carriage, in a low voice that could not be overheard:

"If there is any more trouble, let us know. You are aware we are ready to help you."

She looked up at him for a moment, and he could see the unhappiness in her eyes.

Then because it was impossible to speak, she stepped

into the Marquis's comfortable carriage, Jimmy climbed in beside her, and Hunter jumped in to sit on the seat opposite them.

The footmen shut the door and the horses started off immediately, Jimmy waving as they did so.

Mimosa, however, could only stare at the Marquis, who was standing half-way up the steps which led to the front door, seeing him blurred and indistinct because of her tears.

Then they were crossing the bridge over the lake and Heron was being left behind.

The Marquis did not wait to see the last of the carriage moving under the oak trees.

Instead, he walked back into the Hall and as Charles joined him he said sharply:

"Are you ready? You must be aware that the sooner we get away from here the better."

"I am ready," Charles replied. "But I am sorry for those poor young things having to go through the farce of pretending they are sorry that devil is dead, while nobody except us has any idea of his criminal intentions."

The Marquis moved away from his friend into his Study to pick up some papers from his desk.

As he did so Charles, who had followed him, said:

"I suppose they will be all right?"

"Why should they not be?" the Marquis asked in an irritated tone.

"They seem so helpless," Charles replied, "and I suppose you realise that Mimosa is in love with you?"

For a moment there was silence, then the Marquis ejaculated:

"Nonsense! She is only a child!"

"She may look like one," Charles replied, "but as you are well aware, she is an extremely intelligent young woman with the natural feelings of one, and, of course, it is not surprising she has lost her heart to you."

"She will get over it."

There was silence again until Charles said:

"I should have thought, considering all you have been through together, although I suppose it would be surprising, that you might have developed a tenderness for her."

"My dear Charles," the Marquis said scathingly, "surely you must realise that I could have nothing in common with a young girl who is really only a pretty 'country bumpkin'?"

As he spoke he picked up his papers and walked resolutely into the Hall without even looking back and down the steps to where his Phaeton was waiting.

With a somewhat surprised expression on his face Charles followed. As he faced the Marquis he saw he was scowling and he had the feeling that their drive to London was not going to be particularly congenial.

He however said nothing, but sat back, wondering as he did so, whether Mimosa was, at the moment, still as unhappy as she had looked when she drove away in the Marquis's carriage.

* * *

Mimosa sat in silence, but Jimmy complained petulantly as they drove through the drive gates:

"Why must we go home, Mimosa? How did Cousin Norton have an accident? Why could we not stay longer at Heron? I wanted to ride the Marquis's horses on his race-course and fish in the lake."

His sister did not answer, and after a moment he went on:

"It is not fair that he should have so much when we have so little! It is no use your telling me I am lucky to have Buster and Silver to ride, for they are old and slow, when I want a fast horse."

"I know . . . I understand," Mimosa said in a strangled voice, "but I do not . . . think we can . . . afford them."

"Why not?" Jimmy asked. "Now that Grandpapa is dead and I am the Earl, I am sure we can find some money, as Papa would have done if he had been alive."

Mimosa turned her face to look at him.

"Jimmy!" she exclaimed in a different voice from the one she had used before. "You have given me an idea!"

"What is it?" Jimmy asked.

"I have just remembered that at breakfast Major Toddington said Sir Alexander Barclay was back in London, and you know who he is?"

"No, who is he?" Jimmy asked without much curiosity because he was still thinking of his horses.

"He was Papa's General, and I remember Papa saying what a splendid man he was."

"I do not suppose he will give me a decent horse to ride," Jimmy said gloomily.

"But that, I think indirectly, is what he might be able to do," Mimosa answered.

"How?" Jimmy asked.

"I was thinking when I was at Heron," Mimosa replied, "how well the estate is run and how extensively it is cultivated, so very different from ours, or rather yours, Jimmy, which has been sadly neglected and has gone to rack and ruin."

Jimmy was listening to her, trying to understand what she was saying, and she went on:

"I will tell you what we are going to do. We are going to London!"

"To London?" Jimmy exclaimed in astonishment. "Why should we do that?"

"We are going to see Sir Alexander Barclay and ask him if he knows of somebody who could manage the estate for you until you are old enough to manage it yourself. Somebody clever who I am sure will find ways of making it profitable as it ought to be."

"Do you think I will then be able to have some horses?" Jimmy asked, harping on the subject in which he was most interested.

"Yes, I am sure of it," Mimosa answered. "You can have horses, we can do up the house and have young servants instead of those old ones, many of whom should have been pensioned off long ago!"

"If that is what Papa's General could do for us," Jimmy said, "then let us go and see him quickly!"

"We will," Mimosa promised, "as soon as Cousin Norton has been buried."

*   *   *

It was a week later when Mimosa and Jimmy set out for London.

As it was a fairly short distance, Mimosa decided they could be extravagant enough to hire a Post Chaise, feeling their own horses would find the journey too much for them.

They therefore left home after an early luncheon, as Mimosa wished to call first on Sir Alexander Barclay before they went to Petersfield House in Brook Street, where it might be necessary for her and Jimmy to stay.

As the house had not been open for at least ten years, and there were only two old caretakers in charge of it, she did not expect that they would be at all welcome or comfortable.

In fact, she had decided in her own mind that if Sir Alexander was not cooperative, they would return to the country the same afternoon.

She knew it was not correct to call on any fashionable person before three o'clock in the afternoon, and it was exactly two minutes before three when the Post Chaise drew up outside 60 Park Street.

Mimosa felt rather nervous, in case she was not welcomed by Sir Alexander.

And yet she was sure he would remember her father and, when she explained the predicament they were in, would be ready to help them.

She told the Post Chaise to wait as she and Jimmy raised the silver knocker on the rather impressive front door.

It was opened by an elderly servant who looked exactly, Mimosa thought, as a family butler should.

There were two footmen in attendance and, because of the smart way in which they held themselves, she was certain had been soldiers in her father's Regiment.

"Would you ask Sir Alexander Barclay if he would be kind enough to receive the Earl of Petersfield and Lady Mimosa Field?" she asked in her soft voice.

"Her Ladyship's receiving this afternoon," the butler replied, "so I'll announce you, M'Lady."

Mimosa looked a little surprised, as she had not realised that Sir Alexander had a wife.

She and Jimmy followed the butler across the narrow

but well-furnished Hall and heard him announce in sten-
torian tones:

"Lady Mimosa Field, and the Earl of Petersfield,
M'Lady!"

For a moment Mimosa found it difficult to breathe.

Then she saw at the end of an attractively furnished
room with the sunshine coming through the windows two
people, and as she looked first at Sir Alexander she
thought he looked exactly as she had expected him to
do.

Middle-aged, with hair that was going grey at the
temples, he was a handsome man and had the air of one
who was used to command.

As they advanced it was he who moved first, asking
in a deep voice:

"Can you really be the children of Julian Field, who
served in my Regiment?"

"He was our father," Mimosa answered.

The lady who had also risen to come towards them
gave a sudden cry.

"Julian's children! I intended to come to find you as
soon as we returned to London, and now you are here!"

Also grey-haired, Lady Barclay was, however, still a
very attractive woman and, as Mimosa realised as soon
as she looked at her, exceedingly smartly dressed.

She held out both hands to Mimosa, then to Jimmy
and said:

"How can we be so fortunate that you should call on
us so soon after our arrival? And how is your mother?"

"Mama . . . is dead," Mimosa replied.

"Oh, my dear, I am so sorry!" Lady Barclay exclaimed. "I had no idea of it. As you probably know, we
have been in Paris and are very much out of touch with

what has been happening in England."

"Suppose we sit down," Sir Alexander interrupted, "and you can tell my wife and me why you are here. I feel there must be some special reason, apart from the fact that we are delighted to meet you."

They sat down as Sir Alexander suggested and Mimosa said:

"When I learned a week ago from *The Times* that you had arrived in London, I thought because Papa had been so fond of you and spoke about you so often that you might be able to help my brother."

"But of course we will help if it is possible," Lady Barclay said. "I expect you know that your father, of whom we were very, very fond, saved my husband's life?"

"No . . . I did not know . . . that," Mimosa murmured.

"Well, he did," Lady Barclay smiled, "and you can imagine how grateful I am, and how sad I feel that he did not live so that I could express my gratitude for his bravery."

"How did Papa save your life, sir?" Jimmy interposed.

"I will tell you about that another time," Sir Alexander replied. "First I want to know from your sister how I can help you."

He looked at Mimosa, who after a moment said a little hesitatingly:

"I—I read in the newspapers how many . . . men are being . . . discharged from the Services . . . and how difficult it is for them . . . to find employment. I . . . thought therefore that you might be . . . able to recommend somebody who could manage the estate for Jimmy until he is old enough to cope with it himself."

"We want to make some money," Jimmy chipped in,

"so that I can have horses, really good horses to ride. Because Grandpapa was so old everything has been very neglected."

"That is true," Mimosa added before Sir Alexander could speak. "Our grandfather was ninety when he died a short while ago, and as he was very ill during the last years of his life, everything has been, I am afraid, sadly neglected."

"You have no relatives living with you?" Lady Barclay enquired in a sympathetic voice. "No chaperon?"

Mimosa shook her head.

"I suppose . . . really I should have one," she replied, "but there has been no time to consider it . . . nor is there much . . . money with which to pay . . . for her services."

"How old are you?" Lady Barclay asked unexpectedly.

"I am . . . eighteen," Mimosa replied.

"My dear, you should by this time have made your curtsy at Buckingham Palace and enjoyed a Season in London."

Mimosa laughed.

"That has been quite impossible. There is no money for frivolities."

As she spoke she thought Lady Barclay glanced at her cheap travelling-gown and old-fashioned cape, and she knew what a contrast they made to the elegance of the older woman.

Lady Barclay looked at her husband.

"Alexander," she said, "we have to do something for these children and I have a feeling you are thinking the same."

Sir Alexander smiled.

"You know I will agree to whatever you suggest, my darling."

"What I am going to suggest," Lady Barclay said to Mimosa, "is that while my husband finds somebody to look after your brother's estate, and I know he will find exactly the person you require, you both stay here with us!"

Mimosa looked wide-eyed but she said nothing as Lady Barclay went on:

"It is the very least we can do for Julian Field's daughter to introduce her to the Social World and in that way pay back a little the enormous debt of gratitude we owe him."

Mimosa stared at Lady Barclay as if she had not heard her aright. Then she said:

"Do you mean . . . do you really mean . . . ?"

"I mean," Lady Barclay replied, "that anyone who is as beautiful as you, my dear, should shine like a star in the Social firmament and, while we can leave your brother's estate and the horses he requires to my husband, you and I will see if London can provide the beautiful clothes that make women look like Birds of Paradise!"

* * *

Mimosa went to bed that night in a very comfortable room at the back of the house in Park Street where, as Lady Barclay said, she would not be disturbed by the noise of the traffic, and felt once again that she was dreaming.

Sir Alexander and his wife had taken charge in almost the same way that the Marquis had when she had gone to him for help.

They had sent the Post Chaise away and she, Jimmy,

and Hunter had moved into the house in Park Street so smoothly it was almost as if the rooms had been waiting for their arrival.

While Jimmy talked excitedly and, Mimosa noticed, without the least shyness to Sir Alexander, Lady Barclay said to her:

"You are just as lovely as your mother. I remember when I first saw her I thought she was the most beautiful woman I had ever seen in my life!"

"How kind of you to say that!" Mimosa answered. "But after Papa was ... killed, Mama took very little interest in ... anything and grew thin and lined because she was so unhappy."

"I can understand how much she must have missed your father," Lady Barclay said. "He was one of the most charming and delightful of men. In fact, both my husband and I liked him better than any other Officer in the Regiment."

"If only he had lived," Mimosa sighed, "I am sure he would not have allowed the house and the estate to deteriorate in the way it has."

"I am sure he would not have," Lady Barclay agreed, "but do not worry. My husband loves managing things and will set the wheels in motion to make sure that your brother's inheritance is looked after as it should be."

"You are so kind," Mimosa said. "Since Mama died I have often been ... lonely ... and there has been ... no one to talk to or ... advise me."

"Now that is all over," Lady Barclay replied, "and I want you to have no troubles except how to make yourself look as beautiful, if not more beautiful, than your mother and take London by storm!"

She gave a little laugh as she added:

"I was wondering what I would do with myself now that my husband has virtually retired, although he has what might be called an 'armchair' position at the War Office. But you have given me a great deal to do, for which I am very grateful."

"I would not wish to impose on you," Mimosa said, feeling she had uttered the same words to the Marquis, "and I feel it is quite wrong . . . that you should give me such beautiful clothes . . . as I do not . . . see how I could manage to . . . pay for them."

"They are a present not to you, my dear, but to your father," Lady Barclay replied, "and as I thank him every day when I say my prayers for saving my beloved husband's life, you can imagine that where such feelings are concerned, money is of little importance."

She glanced at Mimosa and said:

"I can see you are still worrying, so let me tell you, although it sounds rather boastful, that I happen to be a very rich woman and can easily afford every penny I am going to spend, and a great deal more besides! So, now smile again, my dear, because it makes you look so very lovely."

Her words made Mimosa remember that the Marquis had told her to smile, and she wondered if he would ever know how lucky she and Jimmy had been to find the Barclays or, indeed, if he would be at all interested.

It struck her when she was fitting the clothes that Lady Barclay was buying for her from the most expensive dressmakers, and that while she had longed for just one gown in which the Marquis would admire her, she was now acquiring dozens.

But, she thought unhappily, there was no likelihood of her ever meeting him.

As she looked at her reflection in the mirror, she

realised for the first time what a good figure she had and what a difference clothes made to her whole appearance.

She found herself longing with an intensity that was a physical pain that the Marquis could see her wearing them.

Then she told herself it was doubtful, in fact extremely improbable, that it would make any difference anyway.

She had learned from Henson exactly the type of beautiful women with whom he spent his time when he was in London, and she was aware that they were very much older than she was and had a sophistication and polish which no number of pretty gowns could give her.

"How can I be witty and amusing when I do not know what interests him or what really makes him laugh?" she asked herself.

She felt despairingly that whether she was in the country or in London she would never see him again.

He had come into her life and filled it, and had saved Jimmy and herself.

But she remembered he had obviously been only too glad to be rid of them very quickly when Norton Field was dead, without even giving her time to thank him for what he had done.

She had written to him as soon as she got home a stiff, stilted little letter which she thought very immature and, in fact, when she read it through, dull.

She had sent a groom with it to Heron, knowing it would be forwarded to the Marquis in London.

She wondered if he would be interested when he read it, and told herself that he would doubtless glance at it perfunctorily, then throw it into the waste-paper basket.

'He came into my life like a meteor,' she thought, 'and now he has vanished and I am all alone and exactly as I was before.'

That, she knew, was not quite true, for she had Lady Barclay.

But it was not the same as listening to the Marquis's deep voice giving orders, or feeling his arms holding her protectively as he had when she had ridden back to Heron on the front of his saddle.

"I love you!" she whispered in the darkness of her bedroom every night.

Then because she could not help it she would cry herself to sleep.

While Jimmy went with Sir Alexander to Tattersall's, visited Vauxhall Gardens and the Tower of London, and watched a military parade in Hyde Park, Mimosa had fittings for her gowns.

She was given bonnets from the smartest milliner in the whole of Bond Street and visited other shops for gloves, handbags, shoes, and what seemed to her a million other things which Lady Barclay assured her were absolutely essential for a young Lady of Quality.

"How can I want so much?" she asked not once, but a thousand times.

Lady Barclay merely laughed and said she was quite certain that a month from now Mimosa would be saying she had nothing to wear.

Lady Barclay had insisted that she should not appear in public until she was properly dressed.

"I am producing you, my dear," she said with satisfaction, "as if I were a magician, which is what I intend to be, and I am longing to see the expression on my friends' faces when they first see you."

"Suppose they . . . ignore me and you are . . . disappointed?" Mimosa murmured.

"You cannot have looked in your mirror lately," Lady Barclay replied.

It was certainly a very different reflection from anything Mimosa had seen there before.

The most expensive and sought-after hairdresser in the whole of London had, with Lady Barclay, studied her face from every angle before deciding what style would suit her best.

Now she thought it looked deceptively simple and at the same time was extremely becoming, and she could not imagine why she had never thought of arranging it that way herself.

"There is no other lady in the whole of the *Beau Monde* who will look as sensational as you, M'Lady," the hairdresser said.

Although Mimosa laughed at herself for thinking so, she had the feeling he was speaking with complete sincerity.

The greatest problem, and a very important one according to Lady Barclay, was to decide where and when she should make her first appearance and create the greatest sensation.

Mimosa understood that from the many invitations which were now flowing into Park Street she must decide which one she would accept for herself and her husband, when "the friend who is staying with us," could best appear for the first time.

This was, of course, Mimosa.

"What if they do not want me?" she asked.

Lady Barclay laughed.

"You will find that many people will want you once you have dazzled their eyes, and you will receive many hundreds of invitations, apart from those sent to my husband and me."

Mimosa found it hard to believe her, for she had learnt that not only was Sir Alexander distinguished because of his war record, but his wife, who was the daughter of a famous Statesman, was much sought after and admired.

Mimosa was very touched to find that they had deliberately postponed entertaining as they had intended until Lady Barclay considered her protegée ready to be launched on what she was determined would be an astonished world.

"I do not at all mind staying upstairs while you entertain your friends at dinner," Mimosa had expostulated. "I shall be quite happy with a book."

"You might be, but I should not," Lady Barclay replied, "and you must allow me, dearest child, to do things my own way. In fact, I am enjoying myself more than I can possibly tell you. As it happens, I love shopping, but I bought myself so many gowns when I was in Paris that I really had no excuse to patronise the shops in Bond Street until you appeared."

Jimmy was enjoying himself too.

Sir Alexander provided him with a fine horse from his stables at the back of the house in Park Street, and they rode every morning in the Park.

"It is not as good as riding over the race-course at Heron," Jimmy said to Mimosa, "but very, very much better than putting up at home with those poor old donkeys which were all we had to ride!"

"Things will be much better in the future when we go back," Mimosa promised. "Sir Alexander has already found two men, either of whom he tells me might well be the manager we are looking for. And, Jimmy, however much fun it is to be here, we must go home sometime."

"Yes, I suppose so!" Jimmy agreed, but doubtfully, and Mimosa found herself wondering if he would ever settle down again.

Because she was obviously worried, Lady Barclay asked the reason.

"My dear child," she said, "do leave everything in my husband's hands. He has already been talking to me about a Tutor for Jimmy, which is important because I understand that up to now he has had only a Governess, who has now left you, and extra lessons from the Vicar."

"That is true," Mimosa said, nodding a little uncomfortably, "but I did not like to worry Grandpapa about arranging more when he was so ill."

"No, of course not, but Jimmy must be properly taught before he goes to Eton, where your father was. Then he and my husband have already decided that after he has been to Oxford he will go into the Grenadiers."

Mimosa clasped her hands together.

"That is what I have always hoped—that he would follow in Papa's footsteps."

"That is what he wants, and that is what he shall do," Lady Barclay said. "And my husband is so happy to have Jimmy with him."

She paused before she went on:

"It has always been a great sadness that we have no children. I feel Jimmy is the son Alexander never had."

"That is wonderful for Jimmy!" Mimosa exclaimed. "Also, I know he needs a father."

"We think alike, dearest child," Lady Barclay smiled, "so stop worrying and think about yourself!"

Mimosa could not say that if she thought about herself, she thought about the Marquis, and that was something she was trying not to do because it hurt her so much.

She tried to find out without asking directly if the Barclays knew him, but they never mentioned his name, and she had the feeling that the Marquis's friends would be younger and probably more raffish than those with whom Sir Alexander and Lady Barclay associated.

Then finally at breakfast one morning, Lady Barclay opened her correspondence and exclaimed:

"At last! Now this is the invitation I have been waiting for!"

"What invitation?" Sir Alexander asked from the other end of the table.

"I told you, darling, that I have been trying to decide at which party I would launch Mimosa like a well-built little ship onto the social ocean!"

Sir Alexander gave one of his short laughs, but he did not interrupt and his wife went on:

"I was really hoping that the Devonshires would give a party as their Balls are always better than anybody else's. But here is an invitation which I think will certainly be the party of the Season."

"Who has sent the invitation?" Sir Alexander enquired.

"Isabella, the Marchioness of Hertford," his wife replied.

"Lady Hertford!" he exclaimed. "I understand she has become most unpopular. In fact, whenever she is seen in public nowadays, she is hissed by the people!"

Lady Barclay nodded.

"Yes, that is true, and that is why the Prince is determined to show his loyalty and devotion to her by giving a special party for her at Carlton House."

Sir Alexander raised his eyebrows but he did not say any more, and his wife went on:

"This is a personal letter to me from Isabella herself, saying how delighted she is that we are in London and asking us to come to the party that His Royal Highness, 'the dear Regent,' is giving for her personally."

"I am not surprised she is grateful to him," Sir Alexander remarked, "but it only adds to his own unpopularity."

"I know," his wife replied, "and that is what makes it so touching. But it will be extremely smart, extremely exclusive, and that is why I am determined that Mimosa, although it will doubtless infuriate Isabella, shall be the Belle of the Ball!"

"At Carlton House?" Mimosa asked.

"At Carlton House!" Lady Barclay repeated. "What could be a more perfect background for you, with all the beautiful treasures it holds, my dear?"

From that moment Mimosa's head was in a whirl.

If there was to be a special party at Carlton House, she was quite certain that the Marquis, who she knew was a favourite of the Prince Regent, would be invited.

As he was in London, it was obvious that he would accept, and then she would be able to see him again.

Because she was in love, her feelings rose and fell alternately, so that she felt her whole body was like a battlefield and she was as nervous as any raw recruit.

"How can you be so foolish as to worry about what will happen when he sees you?" her common sense told her. "He will be good-mannered and charming, but to him you will only be somebody from the past about whom he has ceased to think, and after he has shaken hands with you, it is unlikely that he will pay you any further attention."

But her heart said:

"He will be there! You will see him! You will be near to him and feel his vibrations as you felt them before, and perhaps for the first time you will see in his eyes the admiration you have longed for."

She was intelligent enough to realise this was just a dream, and she laughed at herself for being so childish in thinking a man's feelings, one way or another, could be altered by a mere gown.

"He enjoyed making my problem a campaign, a battle in which he was determined to be victorious," her common sense continued, "but now, as Charles said, the dragons are dead and I am of no further interest to a man like the Marquis, who has every woman in London fawning upon him."

She could hear Henson saying proudly what a success his Master was, and adding how quickly he grew bored with every new face and was then off looking for another one.

"How can you be so foolish as to keep thinking about him?" Mimosa asked herself, and tried to listen as Lady Barclay said:

"I am determined, dearest child, that you shall make a brilliant marriage, which, of course, you should do very easily."

"I—I have no wish to . . . marry," Mimosa said a little uncomfortably.

"Nonsense!" Lady Barclay replied. "Of course you want to marry! You can hardly spend the rest of your life being nursemaid to your brother and struggling to put his estate in order."

She paused. Then she said:

"By the way, Jimmy said something today which my husband thought was very significant."

"What was that?" Mimosa asked.

"He was talking about your woods and Jimmy was saying how he would love to have shooting-parties when he grew a little older, like your father used to have when he was a boy."

"Jimmy has always wanted that," Mimosa smiled.

"He went on talking about the woods and said that one particular one, I cannot remember its name, was very large but the trees grew badly because it was all on gravel."

Mimosa knew that Jimmy had been thinking about that wood because it was where they had been hidden by their abductors and where unless the Marquis had found them they would have been dead by this time.

Instinctively her hand went down to Hunter, who was lying at her feet, and as she patted him she silently thanked him once again for having tracked them down.

"You realise why gravel is so important just now?" Lady Barclay asked.

"I am afraid not," Mimosa replied.

"My dear, after such a long war there are a great many houses to be repaired and a great many more to be built, and for that the builders require gravel!"

Mimosa's eyes lit up.

"Are you telling me that our gravel is valuable?"

"My husband thinks it might be very valuable because it is so near to London. There is plenty of gravel in the southern Counties, but because it is some distance away, it costs a lot to transport it to where it is wanted."

Mimosa clasped her hands together.

"What a wonderful idea!"

"That is one possibility my husband will explore and I am sure there are many other ways in which the estate can be developed to produce a good income for Jimmy so that he can have everything he wants—which, of course, at the moment is just horses!"

She laughed before she said:

"Now that we have disposed of Jimmy, we must think of you and whom you shall marry."

"Oh, please, I do not wish to marry anybody!"

As she spoke she realised that because she was lying, the colour flooded into her face, and she only hoped Lady Barclay did not notice it.

"Now you are talking sheer rubbish!" Lady Barclay said. "I have every intention of finding you a charming, delightful, and very rich husband, and, of course, somebody of distinction. With your looks he should at least be a Duke!"

Mimosa laughed.

"You are aiming much too high, and I am sure any Duke would want somebody far more important than me, and with a large dowry!"

Lady Barclay gave a little sigh.

"Of course, dearest, it is sad that you are not an heiress, but it would not be fair, would it, if you had both looks and money!"

Mimosa did not reply, and Lady Barclay said cheerfully:

"We have only to remember the Gunning sisters, who arrived in London so poor that they had only one gown between them! Yet one married the Earl of Coventry, and the elder became known as 'The Double Duchess' because she married two Dukes!"

"I do not want even one!" Mimosa murmured.

But she knew as she spoke that Lady Barclay was not listening, and if she told the truth, she wanted a Marquis!

A Marquis who was so far out of reach that she might just as well say she wished to marry the Man in the Moon.

chapter seven

When Mimosa was dressed for the party at Carlton House, she thought that Lady Barclay was even more excited than she was.

Her gown was beautiful. It had come from the most expensive dressmaker in London and, Mimosa thought, reminded her of the moonlight on the lake at Heron.

Of white gauze, it had a silver slip under it which clung to her slim figure.

There were ribbons of silver which crossed over her breast to fall down her back like a small cascade and were stitched with hundreds of tiny diamantés that looked like the dew on the flowers.

There were diamantés too on the little frills of silver

lace edging the low neck, which showed the white of her skin and made her look somehow ethereal, as if she were a nymph rising from the waters of a stream.

Lady Barclay had told her when she put it on:

"This has always been my 'dream gown,' but it would be too young for me and I could not imagine, dear child, anybody lovelier than you to wear it."

"You are so kind," Mimosa said, "and all I am afraid of is that nobody will notice me, and you will be disappointed."

Lady Barclay did not argue, but merely smiled, and Mimosa thought no one could have been more kind or have taken more trouble over her.

There were a great many consultations as to how she should wear her hair, but when finally it was swept into a mass of curls at the back of her head Lady Barclay produced four small diamond stars which the hairdresser arranged skilfully on each side of her face.

Finally when she was dressed Lady Barclay brought her a delicate collet of diamonds which she clasped around her neck.

"That is my present to you, Mimosa," she said, "or, if you like, a present to your father for having such a beautiful daughter."

Mimosa stared at the necklace in the mirror and tears came into her eyes.

"You have been so sweet to me," she said. "I only wish Papa could be here to thank you."

"I want no thanks except that you should be the success of the evening," Lady Barclay replied. "Although I know that the gentlemen will be grateful to me for introducing anything so new and exciting to Carlton House, the women will want to scratch my eyes out!"

She laughed as she spoke, and Mimosa could not help laughing too.

When they went downstairs to where Sir Alexander with all his decorations and medals on his evening coat was waiting for them, he said when they appeared:

"I think every man in London tonight will envy me that I am the escort of two such beautiful women!"

Lady Barclay certainly looked her best.

In contrast to Mimosa's white gown she was wearing one of very pale Parma violet and with it a magnificent tiara of Russian amethysts set with diamonds.

She also wore a necklace and earrings to match.

"You look fantastic!" Mimosa cried. "At the same time, I feel embarrassed because it is really I who should be wearing mauve instead of you."

They had already discussed the fact that Mimosa was in mourning for her grandfather and Lady Barclay had said:

"It would be ridiculous to present you in the Social World looking like a little black crow, and anyway, I have always hated mourning. I am sure your grandfather would not wish you to be in black for him."

"That is true," Mimosa answered. "Grandpapa often said to me, 'As I am very old, when I die, do not let anyone mourn for me,' and Mama wore mourning for only a very short time and then only on public occasions."

She thought Lady Barclay looked a little surprised at this and she explained:

"Mama said she knew that Papa was not dead, but simply waiting for her in Heaven. Therefore she was crying not for him but for herself because she longed to be with him."

Lady Barclay bent and kissed her.

"That is the most sensible thing I have heard anyone say for a long time," she said. "So, dear child, we will just ignore anyone who may criticise, and although there is no need to wear bright colours, you look very lovely in white which is perfectly correct for a young girl."

Mimosa knew that the white and silver gown she was wearing tonight had a sophistication which, because it was so expensive and well made, was unlikely to be rivalled by other debutantes, although as Lady Barclay had said, she would not meet any at Carlton House.

"As I expect you know," she had explained, "the Prince Regent has always had a *penchant* for women older than himself, and has been devoted to the Marchioness of Hertford for many years. Unfortunately, however, public feeling is now rising against her."

When they arrived at Carlton House, Mimosa's attention was immediately captivated by the building and its contents rather than her fellow guests.

As she had expected, everywhere she looked she saw exquisite pieces of furniture, many of them from France, and she found herself gasping at the pictures, the clocks, carved mirrors, Sèvres china, Gobelin tapestries, and countless other treasures.

There were also especially fine marble busts, bronzes, and enormous and breathtaking chandeliers.

They walked slowly up the staircase where there were two connecting Drawing-Rooms before they saw their host and beside him the lady for whom the party was being given.

The Prince Regent looked exactly as Mimosa had expected, except that he was even fatter than the cartoons had depicted him.

As he smiled at her when she curtsied to him, she felt

at once the impact of his charm and knew that all that had been said about him was not exaggerated.

"Thank you, Lady Barclay," the Regent said, "for bringing me such a delightful and lovely addition to my party."

He was still holding Mimosa's hand as he spoke, and as she blushed at the compliment he repeated:

"Lovely! Absolutely lovely!"

It was not surprising that the Marchioness, though she was extremely gushing to her friend, Lady Barclay, was very much colder towards Mimosa.

Isabella Hertford was a very rich, handsome, stately woman of ample proportions.

It had astonished everybody when she became the favourite of the Regent, for she had already been a grand-mother for more than twelve years and those who were jealous of her averred that she "looked her age."

It was Lady Stafford who had commented:

"Elderly Dames seem to be to His Royal Highness's taste!"

But those close to the Regent understood that his strange, somewhat complex character made him need to be dominated by an authoritarian woman older than him-self.

As, however, his infatuation with Lady Hertford be-gan in 1806, it was not surprising that now, eleven years later, it was whispered amongst those who were regularly in attendance that the ardour of his affection was cooling a little.

At the same time, because of the Regent's fanatical loyalty to those whom he loved, he was almost fighting with himself to prolong his affection for the ageing woman who had been at his side for so long.

Although she did not say so to Mimosa, Lady Barclay, who had listened during the past weeks to what was being whispered about the fading attractions of her friend the Marchioness, could not help remembering that it was here at Carlton House that Mrs. Fitzherbert had been pushed into the background when Isabella took her place.

Now there appeared to be another elderly woman, who was also a Marchioness, Elizabeth Conyingham, on the horizon.

She was not, of course, present this evening, but Lady Barclay had been told that the Regent had definitely cast his eye in her direction, and the Marchioness of Hertford's enemies were already whispering that her "reign" was over.

There was, however, no sign of this at the moment as she stood beside the Regent and occasionally touched his arm to draw his attention to something or somebody she wanted him particularly to notice.

"It is lovely to see you, dearest Emily," she said to Lady Barclay. "We have heard so much of the gallantry of your dear husband during the War and what a tremendous help he was to the Duke in all the troubles over the Army of Occupation."

"You always say such kind and charming things, Isabella," Lady Barclay replied.

Then, as the other guests were announced, they moved on to allow them to take their place.

Once again Mimosa was looking around her at the beautiful pictures, when she heard Sir Alexander say:

"How pleasant to see you again, Heroncourt! I missed you when you left Paris."

"I was glad to come home," the Marquis replied. "At the same time, I have often recalled how skilful you were in coping with all the complaints and disagreeableness of the French."

Sir Alexander laughed, then he said:

"You remember my wife?"

"Of course!" the Marquis said. "How are you, Lady Barclay?"

"I am also glad to be home," Lady Barclay replied, "and I have brought somebody here with me tonight whom I would like you to meet."

As she spoke she put her hand on Mimosa's arm as she was staring at an extremely fine Titian.

She had been unable to turn around when she heard the Marquis's voice simply because he set her heart beating so wildly that she was afraid he would hear it.

Now she was obliged to do so as Lady Barclay drew her towards him, and as she did so she saw the astonishment in his eyes.

"Lady Mimosa Field—the Marquis of Heroncourt!" Lady Barclay was saying. "A most gallant young man who helped us defeat that monster Napoleon!"

Mimosa could only glance quickly at the Marquis, and as she curtsied her eyes dropped.

Then the Marquis said in the dry voice she knew so well:

"Lady Mimosa and I have met before."

Lady Barclay looked surprised.

"I had no idea of it!"

Before Mimosa could speak, somebody came up to greet Lady Barclay, and she was left facing the Marquis, who was staring at her, she thought, in a very strange manner.

"What are you doing here?" he asked abruptly.

As he spoke she saw his eyes flicker over her gown,

the diamond collet around her neck, and the diamond stars in her hair.

"Sir Alexander...Barclay was...my father's... General."

Feeling desperately shy, she found it hard to speak at all, and the words seemed to come strangely from between her lips.

Then as she looked at him she longed to see the expression of admiration she had dreamed of in his eyes, when she had longed to have only one beautiful gown which might please him.

But it was not admiration she saw. Instead, incredibly, so that she could hardly believe it, he looked angry.

Then before he could speak or Mimosa could say anything more, Charles Toddington appeared at his side.

"Mimosa! Is it really you!" he exclaimed. "When I spotted across the room the most elegant woman I had ever set eyes on and was wondering how I could get an introduction, I suddenly realised I already knew her!"

It was impossible for Mimosa not to smile at the compliment, and still very conscious of the Marquis, who still looked angry, she replied:

"'Fine feathers make fine birds!' But I am still the same underneath!"

Charles laughed.

"That I believe and hope. Do not change, Mimosa. I like you as I know you really are."

"Looking like a country bumpkin?" she asked.

Because she had used the same words as the Marquis had, there was a distinct twinkle in Charles's eyes as he replied:

"That is not the way I would describe you! Undoubtedly a magic wand has been waved over you and now you look like a Princess in a Fairy-Tale!"

Mimosa laughed and it was a very pretty sound.

"I only hope that at midnight I do not revert back to being the 'Goose Girl' in my rags and tatters!"

Then as she spoke she felt her spirits drop for, without saying another word, the Marquis turned and walked away across the room.

Because she could not help it she said to Charles in a whisper:

"What has . . . happened? Why is . . . His Lordship . . . angry?"

"Is he?" Charles asked vaguely. "If so, it does not surprise me."

"Why not?"

"Because he has been like a 'bear with a sore head' ever since we came back to London. Everything bores him and he wishes he were back in the Army."

Mimosa looked worried.

"Y-you do not . . . think it is . . . anything I . . . said that . . . upset him?"

"Why should it be?" Charles asked. "Do not worry about him, Mimosa; he is well able to take care of himself. Tell me why you are here, and where is Jimmy?"

Mimosa told him how she had called on Sir Alexander to ask him to help Jimmy in finding a suitable manager for his estate who might be able to make it pay.

"An excellent idea!" Charles approved. "I am sure the General will know of somebody retiring from the Regiment who might be exactly the sort of man you want."

"That is what I hoped," Mimosa agreed, "but what I did not know was that my father had saved Sir Alexander's life, and because Lady Barclay is so grateful to him, she has given me the most wonderful gowns and is introducing me to the Social World!"

"Now I understand," Charles smiled, "and I am sure the Social World will appreciate you!"

There was no doubt about that, for by the end of the evening Mimosa found herself bewildered by the compliments she received and the way in which almost every man present had contrived to be introduced to her.

When the long-drawn-out and very large dinner was finished, there was dancing in the Music Room, and a great many guests who had not been invited to dinner arrived.

Amongst them were a number of young men who had not sat at the table in the Dining-Room, who were no less eager to dance with Mimosa.

Although she was a little nervous that she would not be able to dance well enough, they all assured her that she was perfect in everything she did.

By the time the evening was drawing to an end she felt she must have danced with every man in the room who was capable of taking the floor, with the exception of the Marquis.

She was vividly conscious of him even while she was dancing and nervous that she might make a mistake.

He was looking, she thought, more magnificent than ever, since she had not previously seen him wearing his decorations on his evening-coat and with the blue Ribbon of the Garter across his chest.

Although she looked towards him frequently, and in fact found it difficult to look anywhere else, she never caught his eye.

She had the depressing feeling that he was deliberately avoiding her and showing quite clearly how uninterested he was in anything she did or how she looked.

Quite suddenly the glamour, the beauty, and the excitement of Carlton House was displaced by a dark fog which seemed to encompass her.

Now all she wanted was to be alone and cry forlornly as she had done every night for the moon that was out of reach.

"How can I be so stupid as to love him?" she asked herself.

She thought the question was answered by the way a very lovely lady whom she had not noticed at dinner was talking animatedly to the Marquis.

She was at the same time looking up at him in a manner which proclaimed all too clearly how much she was attracted by him.

Because Mimosa could not help being curious, she asked the gentleman with whom she was dancing:

"Who is the very beautiful woman wearing an emerald necklace who is sitting at the far end of the room with the Marquis of Heroncourt?"

Her partner looked in the direction she had indicated and replied:

"That is Lady Isme Churton, the Duke of Dorset's daughter."

"She is very beautiful!" Mimosa said with a little throb in her voice.

"I agree with you," her partner said, "and naturally Heroncourt thinks so too. He has as good an eye for a pretty woman as he has for a fast horse!"

He laughed at his own joke which seemed to Mimosa to pierce her heart as if he had stabbed her with a dagger.

Although she knew it was something she should not ask, she could not help saying:

"Is Lady Isme a very close friend of the Marquis?"

"If that is how you like to put it," was the answer, "but I can think of a more intimate way of expressing their feelings for each other!"

Mimosa shut her eyes.

For a moment she felt she must turn and run away from the sight of Lady Isme looking up at the Marquis with her red lips curved in a provocative smile that said more than words.

Then as the dance came to an end and her partner led her into the Chinese Room, which opened out of where they had been dancing, she managed with a superhuman effort to pull herself together.

At the same time it was an inexpressible relief when Lady Barclay indicated that it was time they returned home.

"It is growing late," she said, "and our host dislikes late nights, and I can see he is already a little fidgety. I know he wishes his guests to leave."

The Regent certainly made no effort to dissuade them from doing so.

He complimented Mimosa again as he said:

"You must come and decorate my rooms again, Lady Mimosa."

"I hope I may have the opportunity to do so, Sir," Mimosa replied, "for I have never seen so many wonderful treasures before."

The Prince Regent was delighted, as he always was when anybody praised his possessions.

"I will show you around," he said genially. "You will not forget, Lady Barclay, you must come to luncheon and afterwards I will show Lady Mimosa the latest things I have acquired which I believe are quite exceptional."

"I am sure they are," Lady Barclay said, "and thank

you indeed, Sir, for the invitation. We shall look forward to such a privilege."

Mimosa curtsied and once again she felt the Regent squeeze her hand before she followed Lady Barclay through the beautiful rooms to the graceful double staircase which led down into the splendid Hall decorated with Ionic columns of brown Siena marble.

It was only as she reached it that she realised that the Marquis was standing there with his evening-cape over his shoulders, obviously waiting for his carriage.

Their eyes met, and Mimosa felt for one moment that he was about to walk towards her and speak to her as he had not done so during the whole of the evening.

But before he could actually move a voice from the doorway announced:

"The carriage of the most noble Marquis of Heron-court!"

As the Marquis turned and walked quickly through the front door, Mimosa felt her heart went with him.

*　　*　　*

Driving home, Lady Barclay talked of nothing but the success Mimosa had been, relating all the charming things that had been said about her, not only by the gentlemen present, but by many of her women friends who were too old to be jealous.

"You could not expect a younger woman like Lady Isme Churton not to feel you are a rival for the title of 'Queen of Beauty' that she has held for so long," Lady Barclay said with relish.

"She is . . . very lovely!" Mimosa said in a low voice.

"And she knows it!" Lady Barclay replied. "But I

doubt, however hard she tries, that she will get the Marquis of Heroncourt up the aisle without a violent struggle!"

"A very brave man!" the General said. "I wish all the young Officers were not only as brilliant as he was during the War, but looked after their troops with the same care."

"At the same time," Lady Barclay sighed, "he is one of those tiresome young men who pursue the unattainable, and it is no use our hoping for one moment that he will fall in love with Mimosa!"

Mimosa drew in her breath.

It was what she had been thinking herself, but it hurt to have it confirmed so bluntly by Lady Barclay.

"Never mind," Lady Barclay went on, "at least half-a-dozen young men tonight asked if they could call tomorrow, and it is obvious that from this moment on Mimosa will never have a second to herself!"

"It is all due to you," Mimosa said, "and I am very, very grateful."

At the same time, while she tried to sound warm and enthusiastic, she felt as if a cold hand had been laid on her heart, and tears were prickling the back of her eyes.

It was not until she reached the privacy of her bedroom, however, and a maid had unbuttoned her gown and left her alone, that she was able to let the tears fall and face the fact that her last hope had gone.

It had seemed possible in the lovely gowns that Lady Barclay had chosen for her that by some fortunate chance or magic moment she would meet the Marquis.

He would then be back in her life as he had been when he was saving her from Norton Field.

Now she had met him again, but he had made it very clear that she meant nothing to him.

146

"He is not in the least interested in an episode which he has now obviously forgotten, as I can never forget," she told herself.

Then she thought:

'I will go back to the country. What is the point of staying here?'

She knew that if she stayed in London, Lady Barclay would do everything in her power to marry her to one of the young men she had met this evening or would do so in a few weeks now that she was "launched" in Society.

She knew that however eligible they might be, however charming and important, she would never be able to love one of them and give them her heart.

It had been irretrievably and hopelessly given to the Marquis.

"How can I be so foolish?" she asked herself.

Because she could only think of the Marquis as being as far out of reach as the moon, she pulled back the curtains and, opening the window, looked out into the night.

The garden at the back of the house, which was shared by the other residents in Park Street, was in the daytime a small patch of green grass.

There were a few flower beds, but it had no outstanding beauty except for two trees which gave it character.

The light, however, of the moon rising up the sky and the stars overhead enhanced its charm and gave it a silver magic that on a smaller scale almost emulated the beauty of the Park at Heron.

It was that which gave Mimosa the pain of recognition and a sense of loss that made her feel as if she were drowning in her own despair.

She looked up at the moon.

"I love him! I love him!" she said. "How can I live the rest of my life knowing I have lost the only thing that matters to me in the world?"

There was no answer.

Then as she looked at the bright surface of the moon there was a soft whistle, so low that Mimosa hardly heard it and took no notice.

Hunter, however, who had been lying in his usual place near her bed, waiting to jump up as soon as she got into it, sprang to his feet and came to the window.

He stood up on his hind legs with his forepaws on the windowsill and looked down into the garden, his whole body alert.

The whistle came again, and now Mimosa could not ignore it and looked down to where, standing in the shadow of one of the trees, was a figure, and as she saw it Hunter gave a little whine.

It was then Mimosa realised who it was, and her heart gave a sudden leap.

The Marquis came a few steps farther forward and now he beckoned to her, and as she saw his hand moving in the moonlight she could hardly believe it possible.

There was no mistaking what he meant and she felt it was just like him to demand her presence imperiously.

And yet it was impossible for her not to do as he wished or to hesitate.

Going back into the room, she picked up the negligée her maid had laid out for her on a chair, a very pretty one which Lady Barclay had bought in Bond Street.

It was a concoction of turquoise blue satin and Valenciennes lace ornamented with small bows of blue velvet ribbon.

She put it on, slipped her feet into satin slippers of

the same colour, and very cautiously opened her bedroom door.

There was no sound in the corridor outside, and she knew that by now Lady Barclay and Sir Alexander would have retired to their bedroom at the end of the passage which looked out onto the front of the house.

Moving soundlessly with Hunter beside her, Mimosa walked along the passage and down the staircase into the empty hall.

She knew that once they had retired to bed, the footmen also went to their own rooms in the basement.

"We do not have night-footmen," Lady Barclay had explained to Mimosa soon after her arrival in Park Street. "I feel it is quite unnecessary for them to stay up once we are home, and I hate seeing those young men with pasty faces and lines under their eyes because they have been kept up all night."

"I am sure they appreciate your kindness," Mimosa said. "I have always felt sorry for the night-footman at home who had to sleep at night in a padded chair rather than a bed. In any case we had no callers either by day or by night when Grandpapa was so ill."

Lady Barclay smiled.

"I am sure it is an old custom which should be maintained, but between ourselves, my dear, my husband does not like my introducing new ideas into the household. He feels it is bad for discipline!"

They both laughed, but Mimosa knew now there would be no footman in the hall to watch her as she tiptoed across it and down the passage which led to a door that opened into the garden.

It was easy to pull back the bolts and turn the key, and then Hunter shot out ahead of her and across the garden lawn to where the Marquis was waiting, having moved back into the shadow of the tree.

It took Mimosa only a few seconds to hurry over the short grass to where he was standing.

Then as she saw him resplendent with his decorations glinting in the moonlight, she suddenly felt shy and could only stare at him, her eyes filling her whole face as she realised she was wearing only a nightgown and negligée.

Her fair hair which had been released from its elegant coiffure that had taken so long to create for the party at Carlton House, was now flowing over her shoulders.

"Mimosa!"

The Marquis's voice was low and deep.

"W-why are you . . . here? H-how . . . did you . . . g-get in?"

The Marquis smiled.

"It is not as difficult as it sounds. Charles has an aunt who lives in one of the other houses, and he borrowed her key to the garden gate."

Mimosa was listening, but at the same time all she could think of was that he was there, he was talking to her!

Although she could not be sure, she thought there was a different expression in his eyes from the anger she had seen when they were at Carlton House.

Then because she was worried, she could not help saying:

"Why were you . . . angry with me? What had I . . . done? What could I . . . have said that . . . made you . . . cross?"

"That is what I have come to explain," the Marquis replied. "When I saw your eyes looking at me with that same worried expression they had had when we were together at Heron, I knew I could not sleep until I had told you why I was angry when I found you at Carlton House."

"I—I thought . . . you would be there," Mimosa said, "and I was . . . looking forward to . . . seeing you again."

"Why?"

The question seemed abrupt, and he spoke more loudly than he had before.

It flashed through Mimosa's mind that she wanted to tell him the truth, then she knew if she did so, he would despise her more than he did already.

For a moment her voice seemed to have died in her throat, and the Marquis took a step nearer to her.

"I asked you a question, Mimosa. Why were you hoping to meet me at Carlton House?"

There was a little pause before Mimosa managed to reply:

"I thought that as you . . . were a friend of His Royal Highness . . . you were . . . bound to be there."

"And you were looking forward to seeing me?"

"Yes."

"I have been thinking of you as being at home in the country. I never dreamt, never imagined for a moment that I would see you tonight."

"And . . . when you did . . . you were angry! Why? Why were you . . . angry with me?"

She knew the Marquis drew in his breath before he said:

"I was angry with myself because I had been such a fool!"

Mimosa looked up at him in bewilderment.

"I—I do not understand."

"I have been a fool," the Marquis said quietly, "because I tried to forget the girl I left behind in the country."

"I—I hoped that sometimes you would . . . think of me," Mimosa said humbly.

"Of course I thought of you!" the Marquis said harshly. "How was it possible for me to think of anything else? And yet I told myself I had to be sensible."

"I—I do not understand."

"That is not surprising! I do not understand myself or my own stupidity!"

Because what he was saying seemed utterly incomprehensible, Mimosa could only go on looking at him, at the same time aware that her whole body was pulsating with the joy and excitement that he was there.

She felt as if she had suddenly come alive, that ever since she had left him only a small part of herself had been living, moving, breathing, speaking—almost like an automaton.

For her heart, her soul, and every part of her that mattered had been left with the Marquis, and without them she was incomplete.

And yet now everything seemed to be more vivid, more intense: the moonlight, the scent of the flowers, the beauty of the garden, the Marquis himself.

It all combined to sweep over her so that she felt herself thrill and thrill again simply because he was standing there and she could look at him.

"How can you be so incredibly lovely?" the Marquis asked. "How could I have thought for a moment that I could forget you?"

"But you . . . did not want to . . . see me again?"

"Of course I wanted to see you!" he replied. "I wanted to see you, I wanted to be with you, I wanted to talk to you, Mimosa, and to laugh as we did at Heron!"

"But you . . . tried not to . . . see me!"

"I wanted to—God knows I wanted to!" the Marquis said. "It took every ounce of determination and a self-control I did not know I possessed to prevent myself from posting back to the country to tell you that I missed you."

"You . . . missed me!"

There was a note in the words that seemed like the cry of a bird greeting the dawn.

"You . . . really missed me?"

"I missed you unbearably!" the Marquis said. "But I told myself you had amused and bewildered me simply because you were different from anyone I had met before and that actually I had nothing in common with a girl who had lived all her life in the countryside. I thought you could never adjust to my way of life and my friends."

"I can understand . . . that," Mimosa said in a low voice, "because I knew you thought me just a 'country bumpkin,' as I am!"

The Marquis gave a little laugh.

"Not at Carlton House, when you looked as you did tonight! Mimosa, how could you deceive me? How could you make me believe you were really, as you said, a 'country bumpkin,' and not a Beauty who could turn the head of every man who looked at you?"

There was a note in the Marquis's voice that seemed to seep through Mimosa like the moonlight, and yet what she was hoping, what he seemed to be saying, made her afraid in case she was mistaken.

"What are you . . . saying?"

"I am saying," the Marquis answered in a deep voice, "that I love you! I have loved you since the very first moment I saw you, when you came to me for help and

I found it impossible not to do as you asked."

"You . . . love . . . me?"

The words were only a whisper, as if she dared not let them pass her lips.

"I love you!" the Marquis said firmly.

Now his arms were around her and he went on:

"Your worried eyes have haunted me until I was unable to sleep but only to think and long, as I have never longed for anything in my whole life, Mimosa, to hold you like this, as I did when I carried you back from that damnable horse-box in which you were meant to die!"

He pulled her closer to him as he spoke and went on:

"I knew then, of course. I knew that I loved you and that I wanted to look after you and protect you for the rest of your life. But I was afraid, desperately afraid I was making an irrevocable mistake in marrying somebody who, I told myself, was not of my world and never could be."

Mimosa felt as if the whole of the garden were whirling around her and the light of the moon had become too dazzling to be borne.

And yet she was still unsure, still afraid she was misunderstanding him even though her heart seemed to be about to spring from her body and her whole being was pulsating because the Marquis's arms were holding her against him.

"I love you!" he said. "And now, thank God, I am able to tell you so!"

His lips came down on hers as he spoke, and as they did so Mimosa felt that she must have died and stepped into Heaven because it could not be true.

Then as she felt the closeness of his arms and the insistent pressure of his lips on hers, she knew that her prayers had been answered at last.

The moon was within reach although she would never have believed it possible.

The Marquis at first kissed her gently, as if he were afraid of frightening her.

Then, as the softness and innocence of her lips excited him, his kiss became more insistent, more demanding.

At the same time, he was aware it was very different from any kiss he had ever given in his life before.

As Mimosa had come to him across the lawn, and he saw her moving like an ethereal rather than a human being towards him, with her fair hair falling over her shoulders, he had known that she was everything he had ever wanted in a woman but had nearly lost.

He had told himself at Heron that she was so child-like and, at the same time, so dowdy and countrified that it was unthinkable in his position and his commitments at Court, in London, and in the County for him to have a wife of whom he would be ashamed.

A wife whom he would have to protect against the criticisms and the sneers of those who would not understand why she was different from the rest of his friends.

It was not his own conceit that made him feel like that, but rather his sense of duty towards his position as head of the family, and his obligation to the future generations who would bear his name.

"She is lovely, unusual, and she intrigues me," he had told himself when he thought about Mimosa.

He had known when she cried against him after Norton Field had tried to rape her and had not understood exactly what he was doing, that he was already deeply in love but was afraid to admit it.

Mimosa excited him as a woman, but it was more

than that: There was something so simple and yet so spiritual about her that he could not at first fully appreciate the effect it had on him or that she awoke in him all the chivalry and all the idealistic dreams he had had as a young man.

He had laughed at them when he grew older and told himself it was sheer nonsense.

And yet when woman after woman failed to give him what he really sought, a love that was different from the fiery passion they aroused in him, he grew more and more convinced that what he sought was a mirage, and could be found only in the story-books or in his dreams.

And yet when Mimosa drove away in his carriage from Heron, he had felt, although he would not acknowledge it, that he was losing something very precious, something that he did not fully appreciate and might never find again.

When he was back in London, every woman he met seemed to irritate him in a manner women had never done before.

He had told the truth when he said that Mimosa's eyes haunted him and he had seen them everywhere he looked.

He saw that worried, frightened expression that made her incredibly beautiful, and yet at the same time he could describe her as an untidy, ill-dressed child who was ignorant of all the things which he thought were essential for a wife.

But as soon as he saw her at Carlton House he had been aware of his own stupidity, almost as if it were written in letters of fire above her head.

He had been stunned by her beauty, which he knew outshone that of every other woman in the room. And he knew that the indescribable *chic* with which she was dressed was entirely different from that of any young girl he had ever seen or imagined.

It was then he was suddenly furious that he, who prided himself on being perceptive and on seeing beneath the surface what any man or woman was actually like rather than what they pretended to be, had been so obtuse.

Because he was angry, he told himself he could not talk to Mimosa or go near her while she was at Carlton House, and must see her alone, although he could not think how.

It was only when he was driving home alone that he suddenly realised that he could not go through the night without explaining and telling her that he loved her.

He had turned his carriage round and gone back to Carlton House.

He found Charles, who had not yet said good night, although the Regent was fussing more irritably than before and had even told the Band to stop playing, and Charles had understood.

"I have to see her tonight," the Marquis said desperately.

"You can hardly call at the house when they have all gone to bed!" Charles pointed out.

"Then what can I do?"

Charles smiled.

"For once I have an answer to your problem!" he said.

They had gone together to his aunt's house and he handed the Marquis the key to the garden-gate.

Now, as the Marquis held Mimosa closer in his arms, he asked himself how he could have been so incredibly stupid as not to have known that having fallen in love with two worried eyes, he could never escape the magic of them.

As he felt her body quiver against his and her lips very shyly respond to his kiss, he realised she was giving him sensations he had never known in his life before and which he had not even realised existed.

She was so perfect, so different from what he expected, and yet he could only kiss Mimosa and go on kissing her until he felt as if they were disembodied and no longer human.

They were floating above the earth, enveloped in a Divine light that came not only from above them, but from within themselves.

The Marquis raised his head.

"I love you! My darling, I love you!"

"I think I must have . . . died and now I am in . . . Heaven!" Mimosa whispered.

"You are alive, very much alive," the Marquis said, "and I will never do anything so stupid as to lose you again!"

"You do . . . really love me?"

"I love you until there are no words to tell you how much!"

"Tell me . . . please . . . tell me . . . I have been so unhappy, so unutterably miserable because I thought you would . . . never think of me again . . . and there were so many beautiful . . . women in your . . . life."

"I have never been able to think of anybody but you, ever since I first saw you," the Marquis replied. "It now seems utterly ridiculous that I did not understand and thought . . ."

He stopped.

"That I was not the . . . right person for . . . you?" Mimosa finished.

"That is what I thought, but how wrong I was! You

158

are the only person for me, the person who belongs to me and is part of me. You were meant for me since the beginning of time, as I was meant for you."

Mimosa gave a little cry.

"How can you say such wonderful things? But suppose when you know me better you are ... disappointed?"

"I could never be disappointed in you!" the Marquis said. "My darling, I will look after you and protect you and never allow you to look frightened or worried again."

He felt her draw a little closer to him before he said very quietly:

"You are mine, my precious! Tell me how soon you will marry me."

"Are you ... really asking me ... that?"

"Not really," the Marquis answered, "since I have no intention of allowing you to refuse me. You are mine, Mimosa, mine, because I have fought for you and saved you, and already you belong to me."

"That is ... what I feel," Mimosa said, "but I never thought you would feel it too. And I knew ... because I love you ... that it would be ... impossible for me to marry anybody else."

The Marquis's arms tightened around her.

"How could you even consider such a thing? You are mine! Mine! I will kill any man who tries to take you from me!"

He thought as he spoke of how nearly Norton Field had done that, but he did not wish Mimosa to think of it.

So he kissed her incessantly, demandingly, until he knew it would be impossible for her to think of anyone else except him.

Then as his kiss grew more gentle and more tender,

he thought the most exciting thing he had ever done in his life would be not only to look after Mimosa, but also to teach her about love and to make sure she was not shocked or frightened by anything he did.

"I . . . love . . . you!"

The words came from the very depths of Mimosa's heart, and the Marquis saw that she was looking up at him.

Her face was so radiant that her beauty seemed to be blinding, and her eyes held a happiness that was indescribable.

"You have not answered my question," he said. "When will you marry me?"

"At once . . . please . . . very . . . very quickly," Mimosa answered, "and then . . . can we go back to the . . . country?"

As she spoke she thought she had made a mistake and said quickly:

"But only if . . . you want to. It would be . . . wonderful to be with you wherever it was . . . but I have a feeling I might . . . lose you in London."

"You will never lose me in London or anywhere else," the Marquis declared. "But I agree with you, Mimosa, we will be happier in the country, where we can be alone and talk to each other, and I can teach you, my precious, about love!"

He knew from the little ripple of excitement that went through Mimosa as he spoke that that was what she wanted.

Then with a laugh of sheer happiness he said:

"My precious, everything about you is so utterly and completely perfect!"

"You did not think so when you last saw me," Mimosa

said, "and I know how unfashionable I looked. But I will try to look as I did tonight, so that you will be . . . proud of me."

She hesitated, then she said:

"You . . . did think I looked as you . . . wanted me to look? I was trying . . . so hard to be exactly what . . . you would . . . want me to be."

The Marquis put his cheek against hers.

"My precious," he said, "I would rather see you as you are now! But I know what you are saying, and I was proud, of course I was proud of the way you looked, so lovely, so utterly and completely beautiful and at the same time so elegant that every other woman in the room looked dowdy beside you."

"Do you . . . really mean that?"

"I think you would know if I were lying," the Marquis said. "I swear to you, all the compliments you received were only a quarter of what I want to say and what I feel about you."

Mimosa drew in her breath and said:

"That is what I want . . . and now I will try always to look . . . smart and elegant for you . . . just for you . . . so that you will look at me with . . . admiration."

"I will do that anyway," the Marquis said, "but when you are wearing what you are wearing now, I will look at you with love."

He gave a short laugh as he said:

"Do you realise how often I have seen you in nothing but a nightgown, and how shocked and surprised people would be if they knew?"

"We must make . . . certain they never . . . know," Mimosa said nervously.

"Yes, of course," the Marquis agreed, "but that is how

I want to see you, darling, and it is very alluring when you wear a nightgown so that I can feel you really close to me."

"It is very . . . wonderful," Mimosa said softly, "but I do find your . . . decorations rather . . . uncomfortable!"

She put her hand, as she spoke, against her breasts where she felt them being bruised by the diamond star the Marquis wore on his chest.

He took his arms from her, and she thought for a moment he was annoyed by what she had said, but he merely took off his evening-coat and flung it on the ground.

Then he pulled her back into his arms so that she could feel his heart beating through the fine lawn of his shirt.

"Is that better?"

"Much, much better," Mimosa replied, "and now I can feel you loving me!"

"I will make you sure of that as soon as we are married."

He pulled her closer to him and said:

"I have just remembered that you are in mourning. That will give us the perfect excuse to be married quickly and quietly as soon as I can get a Special Licence."

He felt Mimosa draw in her breath with excitement, but she did not speak as he went on:

"You will not mind, my precious one, not having a grand wedding with bride's-maids and the Prince Regent present?"

"All I want is to be alone with you," Mimosa said, "and have God . . . bless us so that we will be . . . happy ever . . . afterwards."

"That is what we will be."

"I am afraid Lady Barclay will be disappointed, as she is determined to find me a husband, and is already planning my wedding. But it does not matter, does it?"

"No, of course not," the Marquis said. "Nothing matters except that we love each other, you and I. I feel as if I have climbed to the top of the highest mountain to find you, and now that I have, I swear I will never, never lose you."

Then he was kissing her again, kissing her with long, slow, passionate kisses that seemed to Mimosa to draw her heart and soul from her body.

She loved him, and now she knew that he loved her too.

They had found the Paradise she had always known was there in the moon, if only it were not out of reach.

"I love you!" the Marquis said.

Then there was only the moonlight and the music of love which came like a light from them both and made them one person for all Eternity.

ABOUT THE AUTHOR

Barbara Cartland, the world's most famous romantic novelist, who is also an historian, playwright, lecturer, political speaker and television personality, has now written over 400 books and sold over 390 million books the world over.

She has also had many historical works published and has written four autobiographies as well as the biographies of her mother and that of her brother, Ronald Cartland, who was the first Member of Parliament to be killed in the last war. This book has a preface by Sir Winston Churchill and has just been republished with an introduction by Sir Arthur Bryant.

Love at the Helm, a novel written with the help and inspiration of the late Admiral of the Fleet, the Earl Mountbatten of Burma, is being sold for the Mountbatten Memorial Trust.

Miss Cartland in 1978 sang an Album of Love Songs with the Royal Philharmonic Orchestra.

In 1976 by writing twenty-one books, she broke the world record and has continued for the following seven years with twenty-four, twenty, twenty-three, twenty-four, twenty-four, twenty-five, and twenty-three. She is in the *Guinness Book of Records* as the best-selling author in the world.

She is unique in that she was one and two in the Dalton List of Best Sellers, and one week had four books in the top twenty.

In private life Barbara Cartland, who is a Dame of the Order of St. John of Jerusalem, Chairman of the St. John Council in Hertfordshire and Deputy President of the St. John Ambulance Brigade, has also fought for better conditions and salaries for Midwives and Nurses.

Barbara Cartland is deeply interested in Vitamin Therapy and is President of the British National Association for Health. Her book *The Magic of Honey* has sold throughout the world and is translated into many languages. Her designs "Decorating with Love" are being sold all over the U.S.A., and the National Home Fashions League named her in 1981, "Woman of Achievement."

In 1984 she received at Kennedy Airport America's Bishop Wright Air Industry Award for her contribution to the development of aviation; in 1931 she and two R.A.F. Officers thought of, and carried, the first aeroplane-towed glider air-mail.

Barbara Cartland's Romances (a book of cartoons) has been published in Great Britain and the U.S.A., as well as a cookery book, *The Romance of Food*, and *Getting Older, Growing Younger*. She has recently written a children's pop-up picture book, entitled *Princess to the Rescue*.

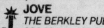